MARIA
or
The Wrongs of Woman

By Mary Wollstonecraft

Maria, or The Wrongs of Woman
With an introduction by Moira Ferguson

A Vindication of the Rights of Woman (Norton Critical Edition)
Edited by Carol H. Poston

MARIA
or
The Wrongs of Woman

by MARY WOLLSTONECRAFT

with an introduction by Moira Ferguson

W · W · NORTON & COMPANY

New York · London

W. W. Norton & Company, Inc., 500 Fifth Avenue, New York, N.Y. 10110

COPYRIGHT © 1975 BY W. W. NORTON & COMPANY, INC.

W. W. Norton & Company, Inc., also publishes *The Norton Anthology of English Literature*, edited by M. H. Abrams et al; *The Norton Anthology of Poetry*, edited by Arthur M. Eastman et al; *World Masterpieces*, edited by Maynard Mack et al; *The Norton Reader*, edited by Arthur M. Eastman et al; *The Norton Facsimile of the First Folio of Shakespeare*, prepared by Charlton Hinman; *The Norton Anthology of Modern Poetry*, edited by Richard Ellmann and Robert O'Clair; *The Norton Anthology of Short Fiction*, edited by R. V. Cassill; *The Norton Anthology of American Literature*, edited by Ronald Gottesman et al; and the *Norton Critical Editions*.

Printed in the United States of America
5 6 7 8 9 0

CONTENTS

INTRODUCTION

by Moira Ferguson

I. General Preface

THE CONTINUALLY growing interest in the life, thought, and works of Mary Wollstonecraft serves, finally, to vindicate her reputation. Scorned by earlier critics, she had lapsed into relative obscurity. Now, however, a more sympathetic audience recognizes her pivotal position in the history of humanist thought.

In particular, her theoretical tract of 1792, *A Vindication of the Rights of Woman*, is nowadays regarded as a crucial early document in the annals of feminism. Her fiction, on the other hand, has had little effect despite its similar ideas. *Maria or The Wrongs of Woman*, the novel she was writing at the time of her death in 1797, echoes and often transcends the notions expressed in the *Vindication*. That this and her other works of fiction have been virtually inaccessible till recently reflects not only a judgment on their value as literature in a traditional sense but indicates, in addition, the cultural preferences of the patriarchal society against which she rebelled.

The subtitle of her final novel, *The Wrongs of Woman*, suggests its main focus. She is at pains in the preface to explain this emphasis. The "wrongs of woman" are the legally and socially permissible acts of injustice perpetrated against women in eighteenth-century Britain. Women at that time had no voice in Parliament; they could neither make laws nor abrogate them. Married women were virtually non-persons. The law subsumed all married women within their husbands' identity—women were *de jure* and *de facto* the property of their spouses. No money was theirs by right. If they were heiresses like Clarissa Harlowe and they married, their money automatically transferred to their husbands. They were denied child custody. A married woman could not leave her husband unless he continually beat her. If she left her husband, she could be compelled to return by law or physical force. Divorce for women was almost impossible. Single women fared little better, and as the story of Jemima the maid in *Maria* shows, women from the lowest social class fared even worse.

Maria or The Wrongs of Woman is probably the first novelistic attempt in English realistically to depict female degradation. Though the work is incomplete, it is clearly articulated and offers a graphic picture of the wrongs done to women. Mary Wollstonecraft's husband, William Godwin, the prominent radical philosopher, collated the manuscripts and edited the work so as to preserve even "the broken paragraphs and half-finished sentences" (of which there are many in Parts II and III). Only Part I was left by its author in any semblance of final form. Although there are several gaps in the manuscript (indicated by asterisks) and even four suggested endings, her meaning is inescapable.

The work stands as a fictional corollary to *A Vindication of the Rights of Woman*. In the *Vindication*, Wollstonecraft analyzes the effects on women—middle-class women for the most part—of a partial educational system where women learn "accomplishments" only to please men. She argues that human rights apply equally to men and women and that, therefore, women should be given the education which will enable them to achieve equality. In *Maria* she depicts in a fictional setting how the denial of all civil and political rights keeps *every* class of women from true fulfillment in their day-to-day existence. Further, she extends her analysis beyond those problems peculiar to women—to the most underprivileged in her society, the poor and the imprisoned, men and women alike.

II. Biography

Ideas of justice and equality were part of the intellectual common currency of the era in which Mary Wollstonecraft lived. The American and French Revolutions, particularly the latter, provided much of the inspiration for *Maria* and all Wollstonecraft's other works.

In 1790 she had openly challenged fundamental beliefs about church and state hierarchies. "Though the enemies of the French Revolution despise the idea of the rights of men," she declares in a review, "yet they are very strenuous to support the rights of nobility; it is therefore evident that they suppose *some* men to have rights, though not *all!* The *few* are entitled to *everything*, the *many*, alas! to nothing!"[1]

In Britain support for the French Revolution and for the overthrow of the corrupt status quo was strong—and nowhere more so than within Wollstonecraft's circle of friends. The group included some powerful thinkers: William Blake, Joel Barlow, Tom Paine, William Godwin, and Joseph Johnson, the publisher at whose home they gathered. Wollstonecraft, who was in Paris when Louis XVI was executed, wrote an account of the early days of the French Revolution. Godwin states in his memoirs that the Revolution produced "a conspicuous effect in the progress of Mary's reflections."[2]

Wollstonecraft's espousal of the Revolution's ideas was undoubtedly influenced by her oppressive home life and her urge toward rebellion. She was the eldest daughter of a former master-weaver who was frustrated in his attempts to become a gentleman-farmer. As an adolescent, she took upon herself the awesome task of defending her mother from her father's drunken assaults. At her mother's death, she took up residence with the family of her close friend Fanny Blood and observed at first-hand the pitiful lack of occupations available

[1] *Analytical Review*, VIII (1790): 549.
[2] William Godwin, *Memoirs of Mary Wollstonecraft*, ed. W. Clark Durant (London and New York: 1927), pp. 50–51.

for women. They eked out a meager living: Fanny painted and Mary sewed until her eyes strained and she became ill. (Mrs. Blood had sewn daily for years to the point of blindness.) Later Wollstonecraft was prompted to action by the severe nervous condition of her sister Eliza. With full knowledge of the consequences, she carried through a plan to remove Eliza secretly from her home, husband, and her baby. "I knew I should be the shameful incendiary," she wrote, "in this shocking affair of a woman's leaving her bed-fellow."[3] As she had anticipated, society censured her for this act until long after her death. Her courageous independence was also manifested in her decision to open a day school in North London, a venture which for a time succeeded well enough to support the three sisters and Fanny Blood.

While in North London, Wollstonecraft had become acquainted with Dr. Richard Price and a group of his friends, including Joseph Priestley and John Hewlett. Price was one of the leading minds in the school of religious liberal philosophy that sought to extend its religious base into secular matters. It was Wollstonecraft's first major exposure to intellectuals with a clearly articulated view of contemporary society. Because of their long historical oppression, the dissenters had perforce united to defend themselves, most notably in the dissenting academies. They evinced a brand of courage similar to that shown by Wollstonecraft in her departure from home, her illegal assistance to Eliza, and her founding of a school. This initiation into non-conformist philosophy marked a new stage in her life.

After the school's closure, Hewlett encouraged her in writing an educational tract, *Thoughts on the Education of Daughters with reflections on female conduct in the more important duties of life.* Her own pedagogical experiences served as subject matter, prefiguring the autobiographical na-

[3]Mary to Everina Wollstonecraft, January, 1783 (reel IX) from the Lord Abinger Collection. These letters were made available through the courtesy of the Carl H. Pforzheimer Library, New York.

ture of her later works. She then went on to read Rousseau's
Emile and other sentimental novels then in vogue. *Mary a
Fiction*, sent to Joseph Johnson in 1788, was the cumulative
result. Once and for all, she rejected her earlier roles as chap-
erone, seamstress, nurse, teacher, and governess. Writing
guaranteed her the degree of autonomy and independence
she craved. Desire and need had determined her ultimate
choice of career.

Her first two works, *Thoughts on the Education of Daughters* and *Mary a Fiction*, though conventional enough in form,
contain many glimpses of ideas she developed more
thoroughly in her later works: her recognition of the con-
straints imposed on women in education and hence in occupation; her realistic view of marriage and her hatred of tyranny;
her belief in the supremacy of reason and the crucial effect of
environment.

About this time, she was invited to be a translator and re-
viewer for Joseph Johnson's *Analytical Review*, and from here
on her writings reveal a growing political consciousness. She
criticized Rousseau's theories of education. To Lord Chester-
ton's pronouncement that women "are only children of a
larger growth" she responded that precisely this kind of in-
doctrination was what made members of her sex "artificial,
useless creatures."[4]

With the publication of *A Vindication of the Rights of Men*
in 1791, Wollstonecraft joined the ranks of the notorious. Not
only was she the first to challenge Edmund Burke, one of the
country's most revered statesmen, but she was a woman. The
publication one year later of *A Vindication of the Rights of
Woman* added further insult to the public injury.

The second *Vindication*—as is now well-known—polarized
British and, to a lesser extent, European intellectual thinking.
She challenged with impunity sacred and cherished tenets of
eighteenth-century society. She horrified a public that was

[4]*Analytical Review*, V (1789): 218.

not ready to confront a progressive thinker who was also an avowed and proselytizing feminist.

All her previous embryonic notions about social inequities are put forward here with courage, confidence, and vigor. She deplores women's social role, especially the traditional female education in external accomplishments that only trivialize the mind. She denounces marriage as an institution definitively oppressive to women. Her sex is "in silken fetters." She urges that educational opportunities be open to all and that women cease to be stereotyped as pretty, vain, jealous, fickle creatures. She denounces writers, such as Rousseau, who have degraded her sex. She cuts deftly and deeply. Overnight she had become, in Horace Walpole's terms, one of the "philosophizing serpents in our bosom"—"the hyena in petticoats."[5]

With the public uproar at full pitch, she put her theoretical concepts into practice by hastening to revolutionary Paris. There she wrote *An Historical and Moral View of the Origin and Progress of the French Revolution,* one of her most neglected works. While writing the history she met Gilbert Imlay, an American adventurer. They soon became lovers. When the Girondins fell in May 1793, and it became dangerous for British citizens to be in Paris, Imlay claimed immunity for her at his embassy. In April 1794, she gave birth to Fanny Imlay, named for her dead friend.

Her passionate letters to Imlay, whose affections for her had now begun to wane, point up a contradiction in her life between dependence and independence. Her childhood and adolescence were quite deprived of affection and caused her to place a high priority on love and security. Her letters to Imlay, together with the *Letters written during a short residence in Sweden, Norway and Denmark,* 1795, provide a record of their relationship. In the *Letters,* she approaches the peak of her prose. Though studded with perceptive political comment, her writing displays an equanimity—unequaled in

[5] *The Letters of Horace Walpole,* ed. Mrs. Paget Toynbee (Oxford: 1905), XV: 131–32, 337–38.

her other writings—attained from a long solitary sojourn in the beautiful countryside. The resuscitating powers of nature enable her—at times—to transcend her deep sadness.

After her tempestuous relationship with Imlay and the two suicide attempts which it fostered, she again met William Godwin, with "friendship melting into love." But she was not to enjoy for long the hard-won fruits of a life dedicated to notions of justice and equality. She died at thirty-seven, ten days after giving birth to a second daughter, who was to become Mary Wollstonecraft Shelley, the author of *Frankenstein*.

III. Maria or The Wrongs of Woman

When Wollstonecraft began her last work, she gave heed to her own injunctions in the final chapter of *A Vindication of the Rights of Woman*, "Some Instances of Folly which the Ignorance of Women Generates." In this section she talks of women "who are amused by the reveries of the stupid novelists who . . . work up stale tales, and describe meretricious scenes."[6] Since pap fiction keeps women from necessary duties, she suggests that they defend themselves against this form of corruption by ridiculing the novels.

Yet it was a work in this very genre, which she had seen as so injurious to women's minds, to which she devoted her final literary energies. Her change of outlook reflected the social evolution of the genre itself. In 1792, when she wrote her first *Vindication*, the novel was about fifty years old. Many women adopted the pastime of reading novels to while away time afforded them by the advent of the "nuclear family"—the bourgeois revolution in family life. Middle-class husbands preferred wives at home: they were status symbols, as were servants. To these women, deprived of outside employment and jobs at home, the circulating library was the coffee shop of the

[6]Mary Wollstonecraft, *A Vindication of the Rights of Woman*, (New York: W. W. Norton & Co., Inc., 1967, p. 272.

day, and the impoverished female flotsam of the revolution served their need for distraction by becoming what George Eliot later termed "silly lady novelists."

Wollstonecraft was alive to this phenomenon. She also knew of women like Mary Astell, Lady Mary Wortley Montagu, and Catherine Macaulay who had written on behalf of their sex and had been ridiculed for their unpopular views. So the idea occured to her of infusing her notions about female oppression into a popular and ordinarily "silly" genre. It was a perfect combination, in theory.

The Wrongs of Woman is her most militant work of fiction. It comes full circle from the ideas in her first educational tract on females, leaving the religious base behind and exposing establishment solutions to women's problems as no solutions at all. This final piece of writing is a compendium of the ideas she had been developing and refining throughout her career as a writer. As Godwin states in his suffix to the novel, "It was particularly the design of the author . . . to make her story subordinate to a great moral purpose . . . This view restrained her fancy."

Yet, as Godwin testifies, the form of the work was a problem for her. Her attempt to create a convincing fictional situation which would encompass and illustrate her ideas was not successful. She knew that her intellectual aim had forced her to make literary sacrifices: "In writing this novel, I have rather endeavored to pourtray [sic] passions than manners. In many instances I could have made the incidents more dramatic, would I have sacrificed my main object, the desire of exhibiting the misery and oppression, peculiar to women, that arise out of the partial laws and customs of society."

Though more unlikely allies could hardly be imagined, she agrees with Samuel Johnson's literary tenets. She does not want to number the tulip's streaks; she is not interested in an individual woman's plight, vividly portrayed with all its idiosyncrasies. It is the history of women in their social situation, the history, in fact, of the female species, which concerns her. The point is "to show the wrongs of different classes of women, equally oppressive, though from the difference in education, necessarily various." An important contrast is that between the problems of Maria, the middle-class protagonist, and those of the maid Jemima, who is so often passed over by critics.

The book often reflects, in fine detail, the complexities of Mary Wollstonecraft's own life. Maria's family, for example, is an exact fictional equivalent of Wollstonecraft's, consisting of a father-tyrant, a submissive mother, and four siblings. The brutality and callousness of the older brother, the father's conduct during the mother's last illness, Wollstonecraft's role as nurse, and the dependence of the sisters are all present in the novel.

The choice of marriage as a central theme is also a matter of re-created life experience. Her family, friends, and employers all led crippled lives from its effects. Her family and the Blood family were both disastrously unhappy. Fanny Blood's marriage, uprooting to Lisbon, and pregnancy caused her death. Her sister Eliza's situation had given Wollstonecraft great anxiety, and court records at the Guildhall Library in London document—as Eleanor L. Nicholes has pointed out— that her marriage was effected under some pressure, with her father and eldest brother in collusion. The example of Lady Kingsborough, her employer when she was a governess in Ireland, had demonstrated the vacuity of aristocratic marriages given over to the vapid social round, with its corollary of child neglect. Wollstonecraft's own attempts to secure a stable relationship, most notably with Gilbert Imlay, were, till William Godwin, utterly disastrous.

The opening scene graphically depicts the effects of marriage on Maria, who is literally manacled in the cell of an insane asylum where her scheming and abusive husband has legally placed her. While in the asylum she is tended by Jemima, who arranges meetings between Maria and Henry Darnford, another unjustly held prisoner. Although his role in Maria's future life is questionable by the end, he does vividly illustrate an important aspect of Wollstonecraft's beliefs: that society is able to oppress men as well as women.

Part I continues with Jemima's joyless soliloquy, Darnford's

narrative, and Maria's story to the point of her marriage to
Venables. Without her knowledge, Maria's uncle-benefactor
has offered money to encourage Venables to marry her.
Shortly thereafter, when her sisters are in financial need, Venables refuses aid. Maria begins to comprehend her folly and
bad judgment. According to eighteenth-century law, her
money now belongs entirely to her husband. "One trait in my
character," Maria exclaims after her recognition, "was extreme credulity; but when my eyes were once opened, I saw
but too clearly all I had before overlooked." (All this parallels
Eliza's naïveté, seduction, and forced marriage.)

The remainder of Maria's story is almost a blow-by-blow
account of Eliza's hair-raising dash from her husband's house
to Hackney. This incident, which lasted only one half hour,
becomes the window through which Wollstonecraft shows
how marriage and husbands can oppress eighteenth-century
women.

Eliza's escape and subsequent dependence on her sister
caused Mary Wollstonecraft to open a suburban school to support her family. Maria's escape ends with her capture on the
Dover road and incarceration in the madhouse. At this point,
though only fragments of Parts II and III remain, it is clear
that Maria's stand in court after her escape from the asylum
was to be a final triumph, a thorough and roaring indictment
of the system which renders women the slaves of men. Much
the way Wollstonecraft rose to attack the theories of Burke
when she was relatively unknown, Maria confronts a corrupt
judge and argues for female equality and justice within the
law.

She delivers an impassioned speech in court about the fundamental injustices to women, injustices which range from
being bartered for prostitution to being legally incarcerated
in an asylum by their husbands. The judge is intransigent. In
his summation of the evidence, he remarks on

the fallacy of letting women plead their feelings, as an excuse for the
violation of the marriage vow. For his part, he had always determined

to oppose all innovation, and the new-fangled notions which en-
croached on the good old rules of conduct. We did not want French
principles in public and private life—and, if women were allowed to
plead their feelings as an excuse or palliation of infidelity, it was
opening a flood-gate for immorality. What virtuous woman thought
of her feelings? It was her duty to love and obey the man chosen by
her parents and relations who were qualified by their experience to
judge for her.

Marriage and marriage laws, then, are Maria's main enemies. But Jemima's brutalization by society is total. Every
imaginable agony and humiliation is heaped upon her. Her
life is a case history of the problems of the neglected poor
generally, and the fact that she is a woman greatly intensifies
her plight. One of the few jobs open to her is washing other
people's dirty clothes, and she remarks laconically, "On the
happiness to be enjoyed over a washing-tub, I need not comment." She could never be a court defendant, as Maria is.
Money is required for that.

The list of specific misfortunes Jemima faces may be im-
plausibly long. But the individual misfortunes were all common and real enough so that she is a compelling composite
picture of the plight of poor women in Wollstonecraft's time.
Indeed, in many ways Jemima is the more heroic of the two.
Her trials are greater and more strenuous, sadistic and more
degrading. She is treated as the scum of humanity, barely on
the rungs of the human ladder at all. But still she refuses to
be duped, coerced or intimidated, though the severity of her
treatment could easily produce a social vegetable. It is exactly
in her independence and personal firmness of purpose—her
"resoluteness" as her overseer puts it—that she is heroic.

It is the will to struggle, coupled with the growth of self-
awareness, which allows Jemima and Maria to tackle the problems facing them. This, above all, is Wollstonecraft's lesson.
But the underlying questions are political and more difficult
to answer. Why does Maria have so little means of redress and,
conversely, why does her spouse wield so much power over
her? What role do institutions play in this? Why are so many

women (assuming Wollstonecraft's vignettes are representative) subjected to the capricious brutality of their husbands in secrecy and penury? Why are poor women so exposed to exploitation? Why, indeed, are women "the outlaws of the world"?

Wollstonecraft raises these questions and more. She also demonstrates the dearth of ready solutions. The judge peremptorily brushes aside Maria's speech. He elaborates on the dangers of such speeches; it proves women should have no power, he argues. He is grotesquely prophetic.

The Wrongs of Woman has serious imperfections: the sheer quantity of the heroines' problems, the lack of subtlety in message, and its technical crudity. Yet this accumulation of Wollstonecraft's life experiences, filtered through the sieve of fiction, offers a .unique exposé of eighteenth-century oppressed womanhood.

As she struggled to complete the story, time and medical incompetence overtook her. Her own words stand as her best epitaph:

All the world is a stage, thought I and few are there who do not play the part they have learnt by rote. And those who do not, seem marks set up to be pelted at by fortune; or rather as signposts which point out the road to others, whilst forced to stand still themselves amidst the mud and dust.[7]

[7]Mary Wollstonecraft, *Letters written during a short residence in Sweden, Norway and Denmark* (London, 1796), p. 242.

TEXTUAL NOTE: The text has been reset from the original edition published in 1798 as Volumes I and II of *The Posthumous Works of the Author of A Vindication of the Rights of Woman.*

MARIA
or
The Wrongs of Woman

PREFACE

THE PUBLIC are here presented with the last literary attempt of an author, whose fame has been uncommonly extensive, and whose talents have probably been most admired, by the persons by whom talents are estimated with the greatest accuracy and discrimination. There are few, to whom her writings could in any case have given pleasure, that would have wished that this fragment should have been suppressed, because it is a fragment. There is a sentiment, very dear to minds of taste and imagination, that finds a melancholy delight in contemplating these unfinished productions of genius, these sketches of what, if they had been filled up in a manner adequate to the writer's conception, would perhaps have given a new impulse to the manners of a world.

The purpose and structure of the following work, had long formed a favourite subject of meditation with its author, and she judged them capable of producing an important effect. The composition had been in progress for a period of twelve months. She was anxious to do justice to her conception, and recommenced and revised the manuscript several different times. So much of it as is here given to the public, she was far from considering as finished, and, in a letter to a friend directly written on this subject, she says, "I am perfectly aware that some of the incidents ought to be transposed, and heightened by more harmonious shading; and I wished in some degree to avail myself of criticism, before I began to adjust my events into a

story, the outline of which I had sketched in my mind."*
The only friends to whom the author communicated her manuscript, were Mr. Dyson, the translator of the Sorcerer, and
the present editor; and it was impossible for the most inex-
perienced author to display a stronger desire of profiting by
the censures and sentiments that might be suggested.†

In revising these sheets for the press, it was necessary for
the editor, in some places, to connect the more finished parts
with the pages of an older copy, and a line or two in addition
sometimes appeared requisite for that purpose. Wherever
such a liberty has been taken, the additional phrases will be
found inclosed in brackets; it being the editor's most earnest
desire to intrude nothing of himself into the work, but to give
to the public the words, as well as ideas, of the real author.

What follows in the ensuing pages, is not a preface regularly
drawn out by the author, but merely hints for a preface,
which, though never filled up in the manner the writer intended, appeared to be worth preserving.

W. GODWIN.

*A more copious extract of this letter is subjoined to the author's
preface. [Godwin's note]
†The part communicated consisted of the first fourteen chapters.
[Godwin's note]

AUTHOR'S PREFACE

THE WRONGS OF WOMAN, like the wrongs of the oppressed part of mankind, may be deemed necessary by their oppressors: but surely there are a few, who will dare to advance before the improvement of the age, and grant that my sketches are not the abortion of a distempered fancy, or the strong delineations of a wounded heart.

In writing this novel, I have rather endeavoured to pourtray passions than manners.

In many instances I could have made the incidents more dramatic, would I have sacrificed my main object, the desire of exhibiting the misery and oppression, peculiar to women, that arise out of the partial laws and customs of society.

In the invention of the story, this view restrained my fancy; and the history ought rather to be considered, as of woman, than of an individual.

The sentiments I have embodied.

In many works of this species, the hero is allowed to be mortal, and to become wise and virtuous as well as happy, by a train of events and circumstances. The heroines, on the contrary, are to be born immaculate, and to act like goddesses of wisdom, just come forth highly finished Minervas from the head of Jove.

[The following is an extract of a letter from the author to a friend, to whom she communicated her manuscript.]

For my part, I cannot suppose any situation more distressing, than for a woman of sensibility, with an improving mind, to be bound to such a man as I have described for life; obliged to renounce all the humanizing affections, and to avoid cultivating her taste, lest her perception of grace and refinement of sentiment, should sharpen to agony the pangs of disappointment. Love, in which the imagination mingles its bewitching colouring, must be fostered by delicacy. I should despise, or rather call her an ordinary woman, who could endure such a husband as I have sketched.

These appear to me (matrimonial despotism of heart and conduct) to be the peculiar Wrongs of Woman, because they degrade the mind. What are termed great misfortunes, may more forcibly impress the mind of common readers; they have more of what may justly be termed *stage-effect;* but it is the delineation of finer sensations, which, in my opinion, constitutes the merit of our best novels. This is what I have in view; and to show the wrongs of different classes of women, equally oppressive, though, from the difference of education, necessarily various.

CHAPTER 1

ABODES OF HORROR have frequently been described, and castles, filled with spectres and chimeras, conjured up by the magic spell of genius to harrow the soul, and absorb the wondering mind. But, formed of such stuff as dreams are made of, what were they to the mansion of despair, in one corner of which Maria sat, endeavouring to recall her scattered thoughts!

Surprise, astonishment, that bordered on distraction, seemed to have suspended her faculties, till, waking by degrees to a keen sense of anguish, a whirlwind of rage and indignation roused her torpid pulse. One recollection with frightful velocity following another, threatened to fire her brain, and make her a fit companion for the terrific inhabitants, whose groans and shrieks were no unsubstantial sounds of whistling winds, or startled birds, modulated by a romantic fancy, which amuse while they affright; but such tones of misery as carry a dreadful certainty directly to the heart. What effect must they then have produced on one, true to the touch of sympathy, and tortured by maternal apprehension!

Her infant's image was continually floating on Maria's sight, and the first smile of intelligence remembered, as none but a mother, an unhappy mother, can conceive. She heard her half speaking half cooing, and felt the little twinkling fingers on her burning bosom—a bosom bursting with the nutriment for which this cherished child might now be pining in vain. From a stranger she could indeed receive the maternal aliment, Maria was grieved at the thought—but who would watch her with a mother's tenderness, a mother's self-denial?

The retreating shadows of former sorrows rushed back in a gloomy train, and seemed to be pictured on the walls of her prison, magnified by the state of mind in which they were viewed—Still she mourned for her child, lamented she was a daughter, and anticipated the aggravated ills of life that her sex rendered almost inevitable, even while dreading she was no more. To think that she was blotted out of existence was agony, when the imagination had been long employed to expand her faculties; yet to suppose her turned adrift on an unknown sea, was scarcely less afflicting.

After being two days the prey of impetuous, varying emotions, Maria began to reflect more calmly on her present situation, for she had actually been rendered incapable of sober reflection, by the discovery of the act of atrocity of which she was the victim. She could not have imagined, that, in all the fermentation of civilized depravity, a similar plot could have entered a human mind. She had been stunned by an unexpected blow; yet life, however joyless, was not to be indolently resigned, or misery endured without exertion, and proudly termed patience. She had hitherto meditated only to point the dart of anguish, and suppressed the heart heavings of indignant nature merely by the force of contempt. Now she endeavoured to brace her mind to fortitude, and to ask herself what was to be her employment in her dreary cell? Was it not to effect her escape, to fly to the succour of her child, and to baffle the selfish schemes of her tyrant—her husband?

These thoughts roused her sleeping spirit, and the self-possession returned, that seemed to have abandoned her in the infernal solitude into which she had been precipitated. The first emotions of overwhelming impatience began to subside, and resentment gave place to tenderness, and more tranquil meditation; though anger once more stopt the calm current of reflection when she attempted to move her manacled arms. But this was an outrage that could only excite momentary feelings of scorn, which evaporated in a faint smile; for Maria was far from thinking a personal insult the most difficult to endure with magnanimous indifference.

She approached the small grated window of her chamber, and for a considerable time only regarded the blue expanse; though it commanded a view of a desolate garden, and of part of a huge pile of buildings, that, after having been suffered, for half a century, to fall to decay, had undergone some clumsy repairs, merely to render it habitable. The ivy had been torn off the turrets, and the stones not wanted to patch up the breaches of time, and exclude the warring elements, left in heaps in the disordered court. Maria contemplated this scene she knew not how long; or rather gazed on the walls, and pondered on her situation. To the master of this most horrid of prisons, she had, soon after her entrance, raved of injustice, in accents that would have justified his treatment, had not a malignant smile, when she appealed to his judgment, with a dreadful conviction stifled her remonstrating complaints. By force, or openly, what could be done? But surely some expedient might occur to an active mind, without any other employment, and possessed of sufficient resolution to put the risk of life into the balance with the chance of freedom.

A woman entered in the midst of these reflections, with a firm, deliberate step, strongly marked features, and large black eyes, which she fixed steadily on Maria's, as if she designed to intimidate her, saying at the same time—"You had better sit down and eat your dinner, than look at the clouds."

"I have no appetite," replied Maria, who had previously determined to speak mildly; "why then should I eat?"

"But, in spite of that, you must and shall eat something. I have had many ladies under my care, who have resolved to starve themselves; but, soon or late, they gave up their intent, as they recovered their senses."

"Do you really think me mad?" asked Maria, meeting the searching glance of her eye.

"Not just now. But what does that prove?—only that you must be the more carefully watched, for appearing at times so reasonable. You have not touched a morsel since you entered the house."—Maria sighed intelligibly.—"Could any thing but madness produce such a disgust for food?"

"Yes, grief; you would not ask the question if you knew what it was." The attendant shook her head; and a ghastly smile of desperate fortitude served as a forcible reply, and made Maria pause, before she added—"Yet I will take some refreshment: I mean not to die.—No; I will preserve my senses; and convince even you, sooner than you are aware of, that my intellects have never been disturbed, though the exertion of them may have been suspended by some infernal drug."

Doubt gathered still thicker on the brow of her guard, as she attempted to convict her of mistake.

"Have patience!" exclaimed Maria, with a solemnity that inspired awe. "My God! how have I been schooled into the practice!" A suffocation of voice betrayed the agonizing emotions she was labouring to keep down; and conquering a qualm of disgust, she calmly endeavoured to eat enough to prove her docility, perpetually turning to the suspicious female, whose observation she courted, while she was making the bed and adjusting the room.

"Come to me often," said Maria, with a tone of persuasion, in consequence of a vague plan that she had hastily adopted, when, after surveying this woman's form and features, she felt convinced that she had an understanding above the common standard, "and believe me mad, till you are obliged to acknowledge the contrary." The woman was no fool, that is, she was superior to her class; nor had misery quite petrified the life's-blood of humanity, to which reflections on our own misfortunes only give a more orderly course. The manner, rather than the expostulations, of Maria made a slight suspicion dart into her mind with corresponding sympathy, which various other avocations, and the habit of banishing compunction, prevented her, for the present, from examining more minutely.

But when she was told that no person, excepting the physician appointed by her family, was to be permitted to see the lady at the end of the gallery, she opened her keen eyes still wider, and uttered a—"hem!" before she enquired—"Why?" She was briefly told, in reply, that the malady was hereditary,

and the fits not occurring but at very long and irregular intervals, she must be carefully watched; for the length of these
lucid periods only rendered her more mischievous, when any
vexation or caprice brought on the paroxysm of phrensy.

Had her master trusted her, it is probable that neither pity
nor curiosity would have made her swerve from the straight
line of her interest; for she had suffered too much in her
intercourse with mankind, not to determine to look for support, rather to humouring their passions, than courting their
approbation by the integrity of her conduct. A deadly blight
had met her at the very threshold of existence; and the
wretchedness of her mother seemed a heavy weight fastened
on her innocent neck, to drag her down to perdition. She
could not heroically determine to succour an unfortunate;
but, offended at the bare supposition that she could be deceived with the same ease as a common servant, she no longer
curbed her curiosity; and, though she never seriously fath-
omed her own intentions, she would sit, every moment she
could steal from observation, listening to the tale, which
Maria was eager to relate with all the persuasive eloquence of
grief.

It is so cheering to see a human face, even if little of the
divinity of virtue beam in it, that Maria anxiously expected
the return of the attendant, as of a gleam of light to break the
gloom of idleness. Indulged sorrow, she perceived, must blunt
or sharpen the faculties to the two opposite extremes; producing stupidity, the moping melancholy of indolence; or the
restless activity of a disturbed imagination. She sunk into one
state, after being fatigued by the other: till the want of occupation became even more painful than the actual pressure or
apprehension of sorrow; and the confinement that froze her
into a nook of existence, with an unvaried prospect before
her, the most insupportable of evils. The lamp of life seemed
to be spending itself to chase the vapours of a dungeon which
no art could dissipate.—And to what purpose did she rally all
her energy?—Was not the world a vast prison, and women
born slaves?

Though she failed immediately to rouse a lively sense of injustice in the mind of her guard, because it had been sophisticated into misanthropy, she touched her heart. Jemima (she had only a claim to a Christian name, which had not procured her any Christian privileges) could patiently hear of Maria's confinement on false pretences; she had felt the crushing hand of power, hardened by the exercise of injustice, and ceased to wonder at the perversions of the understanding, which systematize oppression; but, when told that her child, only four months old, had been torn from her, even while she was discharging the tenderest maternal office, the woman awoke in a bosom long estranged from feminine emotions, and Jemima determined to alleviate all in her power, without hazarding the loss of her place, the sufferings of a wretched mother, apparently injured, and certainly unhappy. A sense of right seems to result from the simplest act of reason, and to preside over the faculties of the mind, like the master-sense of feeling, to rectify the rest; but (for the comparison may be carried still farther) how often is the exquisite sensibility of both weakened or destroyed by the vulgar occupations, and ignoble pleasures of life?

The preserving her situation was, indeed, an important object to Jemima, who had been hunted from hole to hole, as if she had been a beast of prey, or infected with a moral plague. The wages she received, the greater part of which she hoarded, as her only chance for independence, were much more considerable than she could reckon on obtaining any where else, were it possible that she, an outcast from society, could be permitted to earn a subsistence in a reputable family. Hearing Maria perpetually complain of listlessness, and the not being able to beguile grief by resuming her customary pursuits, she was easily prevailed on, by compassion, and that involuntary respect for abilities, which those who possess them can never eradicate, to bring her some books and implements for writing. Maria's conversation had amused and interested her, and the natural consequence was a desire, scarcely observed by herself, of obtaining the esteem of a person she admired. The remembrance of better days was rendered more lively; and the sentiments then acquired appearing less romantic than they had for a long period, a spark of hope roused her mind to new activity.

How grateful was her attention to Maria! Oppressed by a dead weight of existence, or preyed on by the gnawing worm of discontent, with what eagerness did she endeavour to shorten the long days, which left no traces behind! She seemed to be sailing on the vast ocean of life, without seeing any land-mark to indicate the progress of time; to find employment was then to find variety, the animating principle of nature.

CHAPTER 2

EARNESTLY as Maria endeavoured to soothe, by reading, the anguish of her wounded mind, her thoughts would often wander from the subject she was led to discuss, and tears of maternal tenderness obscured the reasoning page. She descanted on "the ills which flesh is heir to," with bitterness, when the recollection of her babe was revived by a tale of fictitious woe, that bore any resemblance to her own; and her imagination was continually employed, to conjure up and embody the various phantoms of misery, which folly and vice had let loose on the world. The loss of her babe was the tender string; against other cruel remembrances she laboured to steel her bosom; and even a ray of hope, in the midst of her gloomy reveries, would sometimes gleam on the dark horizon of futurity, while persuading herself that she ought to cease to hope, since happiness was no where to be found.—But of her child, debilitated by the grief with which its mother had been assailed before it saw the light, she could not think without an impatient struggle.

"I, alone, by my active tenderness, could have saved," she would exclaim, "from an early blight, this sweet blossom; and, cherishing it, I should have had something still to love."

In proportion as other expectations were torn from her, this tender one had been fondly clung to, and knit into her heart.

The books she had obtained, were soon devoured, by one who had no other resource to escape from sorrow, and the feverish dreams of ideal wretchedness or felicity, which equally weaken the intoxicated sensibility. Writing was then the only alternative, and she wrote some rhapsodies descriptive of the state of her mind; but the events of her past life pressing on her, she resolved circumstantially to relate them, with the sentiments that experience, and more matured reason, would naturally suggest. They might perhaps instruct her daughter, and shield her from the misery, the tyranny, her mother knew not how to avoid.

This thought gave life to her diction, her soul flowed into it, and she soon found the task of recollecting almost obliterated impressions very interesting. She lived again in the revived emotions of youth, and forgot her present in the retrospect of sorrows that had assumed an unalterable character.

Though this employment lightened the weight of time, yet, never losing sight of her main object, Maria did not allow any opportunity to slip of winning on the affections of Jemima; for she discovered in her a strength of mind, that excited her esteem, clouded as it was by the misanthropy of despair.

An insulated being, from the misfortune of her birth, she despised and preyed on the society by which she had been oppressed, and loved not her fellow-creatures, because she had never been beloved. No mother had ever fondled her, no father or brother had protected her from outrage; and the man who had plunged her into infamy, and deserted her when she stood in greatest need of support, deigned not to smooth with kindness the road to ruin. Thus degraded, was she let loose on the world; and virtue, never nurtured by affection, assumed the stern aspect of selfish independence.

This general view of her life, Maria gathered from her exclamations and dry remarks. Jemima indeed displayed a strange mixture of interest and suspicion; for she would listen to her with earnestness, and then suddenly interrupt the conversation, as if afraid of resigning, by giving way to her sympathy, her dear-bought knowledge of the world.

Maria alluded to the possibility of an escape, and mentioned a compensation, or reward; but the style in which she was repulsed made her cautious, and determine not to renew the subject, till she knew more of the character she had to work on. Jemima's countenance, and dark hints, seemed to say, "You are an extraordinary woman; but let me consider, this may only be one of your lucid intervals." Nay, the very energy of Maria's character, made her suspect that the extraordinary animation she perceived might be the effect of madness. "Should her husband then substantiate his charge, and get possession of her estate, from whence would come the promised annuity, or more desired protection? Besides, might not a woman, anxious to escape, conceal some of the circumstances which made against her? Was truth to be expected from one who had been entrapped, kidnapped, in the most fraudulent manner?"

In this train Jemima continued to argue, the moment after compassion and respect seemed to make her swerve; and she still resolved not to be wrought on to do more than soften the rigour of confinement, till she could advance on surer ground.

Maria was not permitted to walk in the garden; but sometimes, from her window, she turned her eyes from the gloomy walls, in which she pined life away, on the poor wretches who strayed along the walks, and contemplated the most terrific of ruins—that of a human soul. What is the view of the fallen column, the mouldering arch, of the most exquisite workmanship, when compared with this living memento of the fragility, the instability, of reason, and the wild luxuriancy of noxious passions? Enthusiasm turned adrift, like some rich stream overflowing its banks, rushes forward with destructive velocity, inspiring a sublime concentration of thought. Thus thought Maria—These are the ravages over which humanity must ever mournfully ponder, with a degree of anguish not excited by crumbling marble, or cankering brass, unfaithful to the trust of monumental fame. It is not over the decaying productions of the mind, embodied with the happiest art, we grieve most bitterly. The view of what has been done by man, produces a melancholy, yet aggrandizing, sense of what remains to be achieved by human intellect; but a mental convulsion, which, like the devastation of an earthquake, throws all the elements of thought and imagination into confusion, makes contemplation giddy, and we fearfully ask on what ground we ourselves stand.

Melancholy and imbecility marked the features of the

wretches allowed to breathe at large; for the frantic, those who in a strong imagination had lost a sense of woe, were closely confined. The playful tricks and mischievous devices of their disturbed fancy, that suddenly broke out, could not be guarded against, when they were permitted to enjoy any portion of freedom; for, so active was their imagination, that every new object which accidentally struck their senses, awoke to phrenzy their restless passions; as Maria learned from the burden of their incessant ravings.

Sometimes, with a strict injunction of silence, Jemima would allow Maria, at the close of evening, to stray along the narrow avenues that separated the dungeon-like apartments, leaning on her arm. What a change of scene! Maria wished to pass the threshold of her prison, yet, when by chance she met the eye of rage glaring on her, yet unfaithful to its office, she shrunk back with more horror and affright, than if she had stumbled over a mangled corpse. Her busy fancy pictured the misery of a fond heart, watching over a friend thus estranged, absent, though present—over a poor wretch lost to reason and the social joys of existence; and losing all consciousness of misery in its excess. What a task, to watch the light of reason quivering in the eye, or with agonizing expectation to catch the beam of recollection; tantalized by hope, only to feel despair more keenly, at finding a much loved face or voice, suddenly remembered, or pathetically implored, only to be immediately forgotten, or viewed with indifference or abhorrence!

The heart-rending sigh of melancholy sunk into her soul; and when she retired to rest, the petrified figures she had encountered, the only human forms she was doomed to observe, haunting her dreams with tales of mysterious wrongs, made her wish to sleep to dream no more.

Day after day rolled away, and tedious as the present moment appeared, they passed in such an unvaried tenor, Maria was surprised to find that she had already been six weeks buried alive, and yet had such faint hopes of effecting her enlargement. She was, earnestly as she had sought for employment, now angry with herself for having been amused by writing her narrative; and grieved to think that she had for an instant thought of any thing, but contriving to escape.

Jemima had evidently pleasure in her society: still, though she often left her with a glow of kindness, she returned with the same chilling air; and, when her heart appeared for a moment to open, some suggestion of reason forcibly closed it, before she could give utterance to the confidence Maria's conversation inspired.

Discouraged by these changes, Maria relapsed into despondency, when she was cheered by the alacrity with which Jemima brought her a fresh parcel of books; assuring her, that she had taken some pains to obtain them from one of the keepers, who attended a gentleman confined in the opposite corner of the gallery.

Maria took up the books with emotion. "They come," said she, "perhaps, from a wretch condemned, like me, to reason on the nature of madness, by having wrecked minds continually under his eye; and almost to wish himself—as I do—mad, to escape from the contemplation of it." Her heart throbbed with sympathetic alarm; and she turned over the leaves with awe, as if they had become sacred from passing through the hands of an unfortunate being, oppressed by a similar fate.

Dryden's Fables, Milton's Paradise Lost, with several modern productions, composed the collection. It was a mine of treasure. Some marginal notes, in Dryden's Fables, caught her attention: they were written with force and taste; and, in one of the modern pamphlets, there was a fragment left, containing various observations on the present state of society and government, with a comparative view of the politics of Europe and America. These remarks were written with a degree of generous warmth, when alluding to the enslaved state of the labouring majority, perfectly in unison with Maria's mode of thinking.

She read them over and over again; and fancy, treacherous fancy, began to sketch a character, congenial with her own, from these shadowy outlines.—"Was he mad?" She reperused the marginal notes, and they seemed the production of an animated, but not of a disturbed imagination. Confined to this speculation, every time she re-read them, some fresh refinement of sentiment, or accuteness of thought impressed her, which she was astonished at herself for not having before observed.

What a creative power has an affectionate heart! There are beings who cannot live without loving, as poets love; and who feel the electric spark of genius, wherever it awakens sentiment or grace. Maria had often thought, when disciplining her wayward heart, "that to charm, was to be virtuous." "They who make me wish to appear the most amiable and good in their eyes, must possess in a degree," she would exclaim, "the graces and virtues they call into action."

She took up a book on the powers of the human mind; but, her attention strayed from cold arguments on the nature of what she felt, while she was feeling, and she snapt the chain of the theory to read Dryden's Guiscard and Sigismunda.

Maria, in the course of the ensuing day, returned some of the books, with the hope of getting others—and more marginal notes. Thus shut out from human intercourse, and compelled to view nothing but the prison of vexed spirits, to meet a wretch in the same situation, was more surely to find a friend, than to imagine a countryman one, in a strange land, where the human voice conveys no information to the eager ear.

"Did you ever see the unfortunate being to whom these books belong?" asked Maria, when Jemima brought her supper. "Yes. He sometimes walks out, between five and six, before the family is stirring, in the morning, with two keepers; but even then his hands are confined."

"What! is he so unruly?" enquired Maria, with an accent of disappointment.

"No, not that I perceive," replied Jemima; "but he has an untamed look, a vehemence of eye, that excites apprehension. Were his hands free, he looks as if he could soon manage both his guards: yet he appears tranquil."

"If he be so strong, he must be young," observed Maria.

"Three or four and thirty, I suppose; but there is no judging of a person in his situation."

"Are you sure that he is mad?" interrupted Maria with eagerness. Jemima quitted the room, without replying.

"No, no, he certainly is not!" exclaimed Maria, answering herself; "the man who could write those observations was not disordered in his intellects."

She sat musing, gazing at the moon, and watching its motion as it seemed to glide under the clouds. Then, preparing for bed, she thought, "Of what use could I be to him, or he to me, if it be true that he is unjustly confined?—Could he aid me to escape, who is himself more closely watched?—Still I should like to see him." She went to bed, dreamed of her child, yet woke exactly at half after five o'clock, and starting up, only wrapped a gown around her, and ran to the window. The morning was chill, it was the latter end of September; yet she did not retire to warm herself and think in bed, till the sound of the servants, moving about the house, convinced her that the unknown would not walk in the garden that morning. She was ashamed at feeling disappointed; and began to reflect, as an excuse to herself, on the little objects which attract attention when there is nothing to divert the mind; and how difficult it was for women to avoid growing romantic, who have no active duties or pursuits.

At breakfast, Jemima enquired whether she understood French? for, unless she did, the stranger's stock of books was exhausted. Maria replied in the affirmative; but forbore to ask any more questions respecting the person to whom they belonged. And Jemima gave her a new subject for contemplation, by describing the person of a lovely maniac, just brought into an adjoining chamber. She was singing the pathetic ballad of old Rob * with the most heart-melting falls and pauses. Jemima had half-opened the door, when she distinguished her voice, and Maria stood close to it, scarcely daring to respire,

*A blank space about ten characters in length occurs here in the original edition [Publisher's note].

lest a modulation should escape her, so exquisitely sweet, so passionately wild. She began with sympathy to pourtray to herself another victim, when the lovely warbler flew, as it were, from the spray, and a torrent of unconnected exclamations and questions burst from her, interrupted by fits of laughter, so horrid, that Maria shut the door, and, turning her eyes up to heaven, exclaimed—"Gracious God!"

Several minutes elapsed before Maria could enquire respecting the rumour of the house (for this poor wretch was obviously not confined without a cause); and then Jemima could only tell her, that it was said, "she had been married, against her inclination, to a rich old man, extremely jealous (no wonder, for she was a charming creature); and that, in consequence of his treatment, or something which hung on her mind, she had, during her first lying-in, lost her senses."

What a subject of meditation—even to the very confines of madness.

"Woman, fragile flower! why were you suffered to adorn a world exposed to the inroad of such stormy elements?" thought Maria, while the poor maniac's strain was still breathing on her ear, and sinking into her very soul.

Towards the evening, Jemima brought her Rousseau's *Heloïse;* and she sat reading with eyes and heart, till the return of her guard to extinguish the light. One instance of her kindness was, the permitting Maria to have one, till her own hour of retiring to rest. She had read this work long since; but now it seemed to open a new world to her—the only one worth inhabiting. Sleep was not to be wooed; yet, far from being fatigued by the restless rotation of thought, she rose and opened her window, just as the thin watery clouds of twilight made the long silent shadows visible. The air swept across her face with a voluptuous freshness that thrilled to her heart, awakening indefinable emotions; and the sound of a waving branch, or the twittering of a startled bird, alone broke the stillness of reposing nature. Absorbed by the sublime sensibility which renders the consciousness of existence felicity, Maria was happy, till an autumnal scent, wafted by the breeze of morn from the fallen leaves of the adjacent wood, made her recollect that the season had changed since her confinement; yet life afforded no variety to solace an afflicted heart. She returned dispirited to her couch, and thought of her child till the broad glare of day again invited her to the window. She looked not for the unknown, still how great was her vexation at perceiving the back of a man, certainly he, with his two attendants, as he turned into a side-path which led to the house! A confused recollection of having seen somebody who resembled him, immediately occurred, to puzzle and torment her with endless conjectures. Five minutes sooner, and she should have seen his face, and been out of suspense—was ever any thing so unlucky! His steady, bold step, and the whole air of his person, bursting as it were from a cloud, pleased her, and gave an outline to the imagination to sketch the individual form she wished to recognize.

Feeling the disappointment more severely than she was willing to believe, she flew to Rousseau, as her only refuge from the idea of him, who might prove a friend, could she but find a way to interest him in her fate; still the personification of Saint Preux, or of an ideal lover far superior, was after this imperfect model, of which merely a glance had been caught, even to the minutiae of the coat and hat of the stranger. But if she lent St. Preux, or the demi-god of her fancy, his form, she richly repaid him by the donation of all St. Preux's sentiments and feelings, culled to gratify her own, to which he seemed to have an undoubted right, when she read on the margin of an impassioned letter, written in the well-known hand—"Rousseau alone, the true Prometheus of sentiment, possessed the fire of genius necessary to pourtray the passion, the truth of which goes so directly to the heart."

Maria was again true to the hour, yet had finished Rousseau, and begun to transcribe some selected passages; unable to quit either the author or the window, before she had a glimpse of the countenance she daily longed to see; and, when seen, it conveyed no distinct idea to her mind where she had seen it before. He must have been a transient acquaintance;

but to discover an acquaintance was fortunate, could she contrive to attract his attention, and excite his sympathy.

Every glance afforded colouring for the picture she was delineating on her heart; and once, when the window was half open, the sound of his voice reached her. Conviction flashed on her; she had certainly, in a moment of distress, heard the same accents. They were manly, and characteristic of a noble mind; nay, even sweet—or sweet they seemed to her attentive ear.

She started back, trembling, alarmed at the emotion a strange coincidence of circumstances inspired, and wondering why she thought so much of a stranger, obliged as she had been by his timely interference; [for she recollected, by degrees all the circumstances of their former meeting.] She found however that she could think of nothing else; or, if she thought of her daughter, it was to wish that she had a father whom her mother could respect and love.

CHAPTER 3

WHEN PERUSING the first parcel of books, Maria had, with her pencil, written in one of them a few exclamations, expressive of compassion and sympathy, which she scarcely remembered, till turning over the leaves of one of the volumes, lately brought to her, a slip of paper dropped out, which Jemima hastily snatched up.

"Let me see it," demanded Maria impatiently, "You surely are not afraid of trusting me with the effusions of a madman?"

"I must consider," replied Jemima; and withdrew, with the paper in her hand.

In a life of such seclusion, the passions gain undue force; Maria therefore felt a great degree of resentment and vexation, which she had not time to subdue, before Jemima, returning, delivered the paper.

"Whoever you are, who partake of my fate, accept my sincere commiseration—I would have said protection; but the privilege of man is denied me.

"My own situation forces a dreadful suspicion on my mind —I may not always languish in vain for freedom—say are you —I cannot ask the question; yet I will remember you when my remembrance can be of any use. I will enquire, *why* you are so mysteriously detained—and I *will* have an answer.

"HENRY DARNFORD."

By the most pressing intreaties, Maria prevailed on Jemima to permit her to write a reply to this note. Another and another succeeded, in which explanations were not allowed relative to their present situation; but Maria, with sufficient explicitness, alluded to a former obligation; and they insensibly entered on an interchange of sentiments on the most important subjects. To write these letters was the business of the day, and to receive them the moment of sunshine. By some means, Darnford having discovered Maria's window, when she next appeared at it, he made her, behind his keepers, a profound bow of respect and recognition.

Two or three weeks glided away in this kind of intercourse, during which period Jemima, to whom Maria had given the necessary information respecting her family, had evidently gained some intelligence, which increased her desire of pleasing her charge, though she could not yet determine to liberate her. Maria took advantage of this favourable charge, without too minutely enquiring into the cause; and such was her eagerness to hold human converse, and to see her former protector, still a stranger to her, that she incessantly requested her guard to gratify her more than curiosity.

Writing to Darnford, she was led from the sad objects before her, and frequently rendered insensible to the horrid noises around her, which previously had continually employed her feverish fancy. Thinking it selfish to dwell on her own sufferings, when in the midst of wretches, who had not only lost all that endears life, but their very selves, her imagination was occupied with melancholy earnestness to trace the mazes of misery, through which so many wretches must have passed to this gloomy receptacle of disjointed souls, to the grand source of human corruption. Often at midnight was she waked by the dismal shrieks of demoniac rage, or of excruciating despair, uttered in such wild tones of indescribable anguish as proved the total absence of reason, and roused phantoms of horror in her mind, far more terrific than all that dreaming superstition ever drew. Besides, there was frequently something so inconceivably picturesque in the varying gestures of unrestrained passion, so irresistibly comic in their sallies, or so heart-piercingly pathetic in the little airs

they would sing, frequently bursting out after an awful silence, as to fascinate the attention, and amuse the fancy, while
torturing the soul. It was the uproar of the passions which she
was compelled to observe; and to mark the lucid beam of
reason, like a light trembling in a socket, or like the flash
which divides the threatening clouds of angry heaven only to
display the horrors which darkness shrouded.

Jemima would labour to beguile the tedious evenings, by
describing the persons and manners of the unfortunate beings, whose figures or voices awoke sympathetic sorrow in
Maria's bosom; and the stories she told were the more interesting, for perpetually leaving room to conjecture something
extraordinary. Still Maria, accustomed to generalize her observations, was led to conclude from all she heard, that it was
a vulgar error to suppose that people of abilities were the most
apt to lose the command of reason. On the contrary, from
most of the instances she could investigate, she thought it
resulted, that the passions only appeared strong and dispro-
portioned, because the judgment was weak and unexercised;
and that they gained strength by the decay of reason, as the
shadows lengthen during the sun's decline.

Maria impatiently wished to see her fellow-sufferer; but
Darnford was still more earnest to obtain an interview. Accustomed to submit to every impulse of passion, and never
taught, like women, to restrain the most natural, and acquire,
instead of the bewitching frankness of nature, a factitious
propriety of behaviour, every desire became a torrent that
bore down all opposition.

His travelling trunk, which contained the books lent to
Maria, had been sent to him, and with a part of its contents
he bribed his principal keeper; who, after receiving the most
solemn promise that he would return to his apartment without attempting to explore any part of the house, conducted
him, in the dusk of the evening, to Maria's room.

Jemima had apprized her charge of the visit, and she expected with trembling impatience, inspired by a vague hope
that he might again prove her deliverer, to see a man who had

before rescued her from oppression. He entered with an animation of countenance, formed to captivate an enthusiast; and, hastily turned his eyes from her to the apartment, which he surveyed with apparent emotions of compassionate indignation. Sympathy illuminated his eye, and, taking her hand, he respectfully bowed on it, exclaiming—"This is extraordinary!—again to meet you, and in such circumstances!" Still, impressive as was the coincidence of events which brought them once more together, their full hearts did not overflow.—*

[And though, after this first visit, they were permitted frequently to repeat their interviews, they were for some time employed in] a reserved conversation, to which all the world might have listened; excepting, when discussing some literary subject, flashes of sentiment, inforced by each relaxing feature, seemed to remind them that their minds were already acquainted.

[By degrees, Darnford entered into the particulars of his story.] In a few words, he informed her that he had been a thoughtless, extravagant young man; yet, as he described his faults, they appeared to be the generous luxuriancy of a noble mind. Nothing like meanness tarnished the lustre of his youth, nor had the worm of selfishness lurked in the unfolding bud, even while he had been the dupe of others. Yet he tardily acquired the experience necessary to guard him against future imposition.

"I shall weary you," continued he, "by my egotism; and did not powerful emotions draw me to you,"—his eyes glistened as he spoke, and a trembling seemed to run through his manly frame,—"I would not waste these precious moments in talking of myself.

"My father and mother were people of fashion; married by

*The copy which had received the author's last corrections breaks off in this place, and the pages which follow, to the end of Chap. IV, are printed from a copy in a less finished state. [Godwin's note] their parents. He was fond of the turf, she of the card-table. I, and two or three other children since dead, were kept at home till we became intolerable. My father and mother had a visible dislike to each other, continually displayed; the servants were of the depraved kind usually found in the houses of people of fortune. My brothers and parents all dying, I was left to the care of guardians; and sent to Eton. I never knew the sweets of domestic affection, but I felt the want of indulgence and frivolous respect at school. I will not disgust you with a recital of the vices of my youth, which can scarcely be comprehended by female delicacy. I was taught to love by a creature I am ashamed to mention; and the other women with whom I afterwards became intimate, were of a class of which you can have no knowledge. I formed my acquaintance with them at the theaters; and, when vivacity danced in their eyes, I was not easily disgusted by the vulgarity which flowed from their lips. Having spent, a few years after I was of age, [the whole of] a considerable patrimony, excepting a few hundreds, I had no resource but to purchase a commission in a new-raised regiment, destined to subjugate America. The regret I felt to renounce a life of pleasure, was counter-balanced by the curiosity I had to see America, or rather to travel; [nor had any of those circumstances occurred to my youth, which might have been calculated] to bind my country to my heart. I shall not trouble you with the details of a military life. My blood was still kept in motion; till, towards the close of the contest, I was wounded and taken prisoner.

"Confined to my bed, or chair, by a lingering cure, my only refuge from the preying activity of my mind, was books, which I read with great avidity, profiting by the conversation of my host, a man of sound understanding. My political sentiments now underwent a total change; and, dazzled by the hospitality of the Americans, I determined to take up my abode with freedom. I, therefore, with my usual impetuosity, sold my commission, and travelled into the interior parts of the country, to lay out my money to advantage. Added to this, I did not much like the puritanical manners of the large towns. Inequality of condition was there most disgustingly galling. The only pleasure wealth afforded, was to make an ostentatious display of it; for the cultivation of the fine arts, or literature, had not introduced into the first circles that polish of manners which renders the rich so essentially superior to the poor in Europe. Added to this, an influx of vices had been let in by the Revolution, and the most rigid principles of religion shaken to the centre, before the understanding could be gradually emancipated from the prejudices which led their ancestors undauntedly to seek an inhospitable clime and unbroken soil. The resolution, that led them, in pursuit of independence, to embark on rivers like seas, to search for unknown shores, and to sleep under the hovering mists of endless forests, whose baleful damps agued their limbs, was now turned into commercial speculations, till the national character exhibited a phenomenon in the history of the human mind—a head enthusiastically enterprising, with cold selfishness of heart. And woman, lovely woman!—they charm everywhere—still there is a degree of prudery, and a want of taste and ease in the manners of the American women, that renders them, in spite of their roses and lilies, far inferior to our European charmers. In the country, they have often a bewitching simplicity of character; but, in the cities, they have all the airs and ignorance of the ladies who give the tone to the circles of the large trading towns in England. They are fond of their ornaments, merely because they are good, and not because they embellish their persons; and are more gratified to inspire the women with jealousy of these exterior advantages, than the men with love. All the frivolity which often (excuse me, Madam) renders the society of modest women so stupid in England, here seemed to throw still more leaden fetters on their charms. Not being an adept in gallantry, I found that I could only keep myself awake in their company by making downright love to them.

"But, not to intrude on your patience, I retired to the track of land which I had purchased in the country, and my time passed pleasantly enough while I cut down the trees, built my house, and planted my different crops. But winter and idleness came, and I longed for more elegant society, to hear what was passing in the world, and to do something better than vegetate with the animals that made a very considerable part of my household. Consequently, I determined to travel. Motion was a substitute for variety of objects; and, passing over immense tracks of country, I exhausted my exuberant spirits, without obtaining much experience. I every where saw industry the fore-runner and not the consequence, of luxury; but this country, everything being on an ample scale, did not afford those picturesque views, which a certain degree of cultivation is necessary gradually to produce. The eye wandered without an object to fix upon over immeasureable plains, and lakes that seemed replenished by the ocean, whilst eternal forests of small clustering trees, obstructed the circulation of air, and embarrassed the path, without gratifying the eye of taste. No cottage smiling in the waste, no travellers hailed us, to give life to silent nature; or, if perchance we saw the print of a footstep in our path, it was a dreadful warning to turn aside; and the head ached as if assailed by the scalping knife. The Indians who hovered on the skirts of the European settlements had only learned of their neighbours to plunder, and they stole their guns from them to do it with more safety.

"From the woods and back settlements, I returned to the towns, and learned to eat and drink most valiantly; but without entering into commerce (and I detested commerce) I found I could not live there; and, growing heartily weary of the land of liberty and vulgar aristocracy, seated on her bags of dollars, I resolved once more to visit Europe. I wrote to a distant relation in England, with whom I had been educated, mentioning the vessel in which I intended to sail. Arriving in London, my senses were intoxicated. I ran from street to street, from theater to theater, and the women of the town (again I must beg pardon for my habitual frankness) appeared to me like angels.

"A week was spent in this thoughtless manner, when, returning very late to the hotel in which I had lodged ever since my arrival, I was knocked down in a private street, and hurried, in a state of insensibility, into a coach, which brought me hither, and I only recovered my senses to be treated like one who had lost them. My keepers are deaf to my remonstrances and enquiries, yet assure me that my confinement shall not last long. Still I cannot guess, though I weary myself with conjectures, why I am confined, or in what part of England this house is situated. I imagine sometimes that I hear the sea roar, and wished myself again on the Atlantic, till I had a glimpse of you."*

A few moments were only allowed to Maria to comment on this narrative, when Darnford left her to her own thoughts, to the "never ending, still beginning," task of weighing his words, recollecting his tones of voice, and feeling them reverberate on her heart.

---

*The introduction of Darnford as the deliverer of Maria in a former instance, appears to have been an after-thought of the author. This has occasioned the omission of any allusion to that circumstance in the preceding narration. EDITOR. [Godwin's note]

CHAPTER 4

PITY, and the forlorn seriousness of adversity, have both been considered as dispositions favourable to love, while satirical writers have attributed the propensity to the relaxing effect of idleness; what chance then had Maria of escaping, when pity, sorrow, and solitude all conspired to soften her mind, and nourish romantic wishes, and, from a natural progress, romantic expectations?

Maria was six-and-twenty. But, such was the native soundness of her constitution, that time had only given to her countenance the character of her mind. Revolving thought, and exercised affections had banished some of the playful graces of innocence, producing insensibly that irregularity of features which the struggles of the understanding to trace or govern the strong emotions of the heart, are wont to imprint on the yielding mass. Grief and care had mellowed, without obscuring, the bright tints of youth, and the thoughtfulness which resided on her brow did not take from the feminine softness of her features; nay, such was the sensibility which often mantled over it, that she frequently appeared, like a large proportion of her sex, only born to feel; and the activity of her well-proportioned, and even almost voluptuous figure, inspired the idea of strength of mind, rather than of body. There was a simplicity sometimes indeed in her manner, which bordered on infantine ingenuousness, that led people of common discernment to underrate her talents, and smile at the flights of her imagination. But those who could not comprehend the delicacy of her sentiments, were attached by her unfailing sympathy, so that she was very generally beloved by characters of very different descriptions; still, she was too much under the influence of an ardent imagination to adhere to common rules.

There are mistakes of conduct which at five-and-twenty prove the strength of the mind, that, ten or fifteen years after, would demonstrate its weakness, its incapacity to acquire a sane judgment. The youths who are satisfied with the ordinary pleasures of life, and do not sigh after ideal phantoms of love and friendship, will never arrive at great maturity of understanding; but if these reveries are cherished, as is too frequently the case with women, when experience ought to have taught them in what human happiness consists, they become as useless as they are wretched. Besides, their pains and pleasures are so dependent on outward circumstances, on the objects of their affections, that they seldom act from the impulse of a nerved mind, able to choose its own pursuit.

Having had to struggle incessantly with the vices of mankind, Maria's imagination found repose in pourtraying the possible virtues the world might contain. Pygmalion formed an ivory maid, and longed for an informing soul. She, on the contrary, combined all the qualities of a hero's mind, and fate presented a statue in which she might enshrine them.

We mean not to trace the progress of this passion, or recount how often Darnford and Maria were obliged to part in the midst of an interesting conversation. Jemima ever watched on the tip-toe of fear, and frequently separated them on a false alarm, when they would have given worlds to remain a little longer together.

A magic lamp now seemed to be suspended in Maria's prison, and fairy landscapes flitted round the gloomy walls, late so blank. Rushing from the depth of despair, on the seraph wing of hope, she found herself happy.—She was beloved, and every emotion was rapturous.

To Darnford she had not shown a decided affection; the fear of outrunning his, a sure proof of love, made her often assume a coldness and indifference foreign from her character; and, even when giving way to the playful emotions of a heart just loosened from the frozen bond of grief, there was a delicacy in her manner of expressing her sensibility, which made him doubt whether it was the effect of love.

One evening, when Jemima left them, to listen to the sound of a distant footstep, which seemed cautiously to approach, he seized Maria's hand—it was not withdrawn. They conversed with earnestness of their situation; and, during the conversation, he once or twice gently drew her towards him. He felt the fragrance of her breath, and longed, yet feared, to touch the lips from which it issued; spirits of purity seemed to guard them, while all the enchanting graces of love sported on her cheeks, and languished in her eyes.

Jemima entering, he reflected on his diffidence with poignant regret, and, she once more taking alarm, he ventured, as Maria stood near his chair, to approach her lips with a declaration of love. She drew back with solemnity, he hung down his head abashed; but lifting his eyes timidly, they met her's; she had determined, during that instant, and suffered their rays to mingle. He took, with more ardour, reassured, a half-consenting, half-reluctant kiss, reluctant only from modesty; and there was a sacredness in her dignified manner of reclining her glowing face on his shoulder, that powerfully impressed him. Desire was lost in more ineffable emotions, and to protect her from insult and sorrow—to make her happy, seemed not only the first wish of his heart, but the most noble duty of his life. Such angelic confidence demanded the fidelity of honour; but could he, feeling her in every pulsation, could he ever change, could he be a villain? The emotion with which she, for a moment, allowed herself to be pressed to his bosom, the tear of rapturous sympathy, mingled with a soft melancholy sentiment of recollected disappointment, said—more of truth and faithfulness, than the tongue could have given utterance to in hours! They were silent—yet discoursed, how eloquently? till, after a moment's reflection, Maria drew her chair by the side of his, and, with a composed sweetness of voice, and supernatural benignity of countenance, said, "I must open my whole heart to you; you must be told who I am, why I am here, and why, telling you I am a wife, I blush not to"—the blush spoke the rest.

Jemima was again at her elbow, and the restraint of her presence did not prevent an animated conversation, in which love, sly urchin, was ever at bo-peep.

So much of heaven did they enjoy, that paradise bloomed around them; or they, by a powerful spell, had been transported into Armida's garden. Love, the grand enchanter, "lapt them in Elysium," and every sense was harmonized to joy and social extacy. So animated, indeed, were their accents of tenderness, in discussing what, in other circumstances, would have been commonplace subjects, that Jemima felt, with surprise, a tear of pleasure trickling down her rugged cheeks. She wiped it away, half ashamed; and when Maria kindly enquired the cause, with all the eager solicitude of a happy being wishing to impart to all nature its overflowing felicity, Jemima owned that it was the first tear that social enjoyment had ever drawn from her. She seemed indeed to breathe more freely; the cloud of suspicion cleared away from her brow; she felt herself, for once in her life, treated like a fellow-creature.

Imagination! who can paint thy power; or reflect the evanescent tints of hope fostered by thee? A despondent gloom had long obscured Maria's horizon—now the sun broke forth, the rainbow appeared, and every prospect was fair. Horror still reigned in the darkened cells, suspicion lurked in the passages, and whispered along the walls. The yells of men possessed, sometimes, made them pause, and wonder that they felt so happy, in a tomb of living death. They even chid themselves for such apparent insensibility; still the world contained not three happier beings. And Jemima, after again patrolling the passage, was so softened by the air of confidence which breathed around her, that she voluntarily began an account of herself.

CHAPTER 5

"MY FATHER," said Jemima, "seduced my mother, a pretty girl, with whom he lived fellow-servant; and she no sooner perceived the natural, the dreaded consequence, than the terrible conviction flashed on her—that she was ruined. Honesty, and a regard for her reputation, had been the only principles inculcated by her mother; and they had been so forcibly impressed, that she feared shame, more than the poverty to which it would lead. Her incessant importunities to prevail upon my father to screen her from reproach by marrying her, as he had promised in the fervour of seduction, estranged him from her so completely, that her very person became distasteful to him; and he began to hate, as well as despise me, before I was born.

"My mother, grieved to the soul by his neglect, and unkind treatment, actually resolved to famish herself; and injured her health by the attempt; though she had not sufficient resolution to adhere to her project, or renounce it entirely. Death came not at her call; yet sorrow, and the methods she adopted to conceal her condition, still doing the work of a house-maid, had such an effect on her constitution, that she died in the wretched garret, where her virtuous mistress had forced her to take refuge in the very pangs of labour, though my father, after a slight reproof, was allowed to remain in his place—allowed by the mother of six children, who, scarcely permitting a footstep to be heard, during her month's indulgence, felt no sympathy for the poor wretch, denied every comfort required by her situation.

"The day my mother, died, the ninth after my birth, I was consigned to the care of the cheapest nurse my father could find; who suckled her own child at the same time, and lodged as many more as she could get, in two cellar-like apartments.

"Poverty, and the habit of seeing children die off her hands, had so hardened her heart, that the office of a mother did not awaken the tenderness of a woman; nor were the feminine caresses which seem a part of the rearing of a child, ever bestowed on me. The chicken has a wing to shelter under; but I had no bosom to nestle in, no kindred warmth to foster me. Left in dirt, to cry with cold and hunger till I was weary, and sleep without ever being prepared by exercise, or lulled by kindness to rest; could I be expected to become any thing but a weak and rickety babe? Still, in spite of neglect, I continued to exist, to learn to curse existence, [her countenance grew ferocious as she spoke,] and the treatment that rendered me miserable, seemed to sharpen my wits. Confined then in a damp hovel, to rock the cradle of the succeeding tribe, I looked like a little old woman, or a hag shrivelling into nothing. The furrows of reflection and care contracted the youthful cheek, and gave a sort of supernatural wildness to the ever watchful eye. During this period, my father had married another fellow-servant, who loved him less, and knew better how to manage his passion, than my mother. She likewise proving with child, they agreed to keep a shop: my stepmother, if, being an illegitimate offspring, I may venture thus to characterize her, having obtained a sum of a rich relation, for that purpose.

"Soon after her lying-in, she prevailed on my father to take me home, to save the expence of maintaining me, and of hiring a girl to assist her in the care of the child. I was young, it was true, but appeared a knowing little thing, and might be made handy. Accordingly I was brought to her house; but not to a home—for a home I never knew. Of this child, a daughter, she was extravagantly fond; and it was a part of my employment, to assist to spoil her, by humouring all her whims, and bearing all her caprices. Feeling her own consequence, before she could speak, she had learned the art of tormenting me, and if I ever dared to resist, I received blows, laid on with no compunctious hand, or was sent to bed dinnerless, as well as supperless. I said that it was a part of my daily labour to attend this child, with the servility of a slave; still it was but a part. I was sent out in all seasons, and from place to place, to carry burdens far above my strength, without being allowed to draw near the fire, or ever being cheered by encouragement or kindness. No wonder then, treated like a creature of another species, that I began to envy, and at length to hate, the darling of the house. Yet, I perfectly remember, that it was the caresses, and kind expressions of my step-mother, which first excited my jealous discontent. Once, I cannot forget it, when she was calling in vain her wayward child to kiss her, I ran to her, saying, 'I will kiss you, ma'am!' and how did my heart, which was in my mouth, sink, what was my debasement of soul, when pushed away with—'I do not want you, pert thing!' Another day, when a new gown had excited the highest good humour, and she uttered the appropriate *dear*, addressed unexpectedly to me, I thought I could never do enough to please her; I was all alacrity, and rose proportionably in my own estimation.

"As her daughter grew up, she was pampered with cakes and fruit, while I was, literally speaking, fed with the refuse of the table, with her leavings. A liquorish tooth is, I believe, common to children, and I used to steal any thing sweet, that I could catch up with a chance of concealment. When detected, she was not content to chastize me herself at the moment, but, on my father's return in the evening (he was a shopman), the principal discourse was to recount my faults, and attribute them to the wicked disposition which I had brought into the world with me, inherited from my mother. He did not fail to leave the marks of his resentment on my body, and then solaced himself by playing with my sister.— I could have murdered her at those moments. To save myself from these unmerciful corrections, I resorted to falshood, and the untruths which I sturdily maintained, were brought in judgment against me, to support my tyrant's inhuman charge of my natural propensity to vice. Seeing me treated with contempt, and always being fed and dressed better, my sister conceived a contemptuous opinion of me, that proved an obstacle to all affection; and my father, hearing continually of my faults, began to consider me as a curse entailed on him for his sins: he was therefore easily prevailed on to bind me apprentice to one of my step-mother's friends, who kept a slop-shop in Wapping. I was represented (as it was said) in my true colours; but she, 'warranted,' snapping her fingers, 'that she should break my spirit or heart.'

"My mother replied, with a whine, 'that if any body could make me better, it was such a clever woman as herself; though, for her own part, she had tried in vain; but good-nature was her fault.'

"I shudder with horror, when I recollect the treatment I had now to endure. Not only under the lash of my task-mistress, but the drudge of the maid, apprentices and children, I never had a taste of human kindness to soften the rigour of perpetual labour. I had been introduced as an object of abhorrence into the family; as a creature of whom my step-mother, though she had been kind enough to let me live in the house with her own child, could make nothing. I was described as a wretch, whose nose must be kept to the grinding stone—and it was held there with an iron grasp. It seemed indeed the privilege of their superior nature to kick me about, like the dog or cat. If I were attentive, I was called fawning, if refractory, an obstinate mule, and like a mule I received their censure on my loaded back. Often has my mistress, for some instance of forgetfulness, thrown me from one side of the kitchen to the other, knocked my head against the wall, spit in my face, with various refinements on barbarity that I forbear to enumerate, though they were all acted over again by the servant, with additional insults, to which the appellation of *bastard*, was commonly added, with taunts or sneers. But I will not attempt to give you an adequate idea of my situation, lest you, who probably have never been drenched with the dregs of human misery, should think I exaggerate.

"I stole now, from absolute necessity,—bread; yet whatever

else was taken, which I had it not in my power to take, was ascribed to me. I was the filching cat, the ravenous dog, the dumb brute, who must bear all; for if I endeavoured to exculpate myself, I was silenced, without any enquiries being made, with 'Hold your tongue, you never tell truth.' Even the very air I breathed was tainted with scorn; for I was sent to the neighbouring shops with Glutton, Liar, or Thief, written on my forehead. This was, at first, the most bitter punishment; but sullen pride, or a kind of stupid desperation, made me, at length, almost regardless of the contempt, which had wrung from me so many solitary tears at the only moments when I was allowed to rest.

"Thus was I the mark of cruelty till my sixteenth year; and then I have only to point out a change of misery; for a period I never knew. Allow me first to make one observation. Now I look back, I cannot help attributing the greater part of my misery, to the misfortune of having been thrown into the world without the grand support of life—a mother's affection. I had no one to love me; or to make me respected, to enable me to acquire respect. I was an egg dropped on the sand; a pauper by nature, hunted from family to family, who belonged to nobody—and nobody cared for me. I was despised from my birth, and denied the chance of obtaining a footing for myself in society. Yes; I had not even the chance of being considered as a fellow-creature—yet all the people with whom I lived, brutalized as they were by the low cunning of trade, and the despicable shifts of poverty, were not without bowels, though they never yearned for me. I was, in fact, born a slave, and chained by infamy to slavery during the whole of existence, without having any companions to alleviate it by sympathy, or teach me how to rise above it by their example. But, to resume the thread of my tale—

"At sixteen, I suddenly grew tall, and something like comeliness appeared on a Sunday, when I had time to wash my face, and put on clean clothes. My master had once or twice caught hold of me in the passage; but I instinctively avoided his disgusting caresses. One day however, when the family were at a methodist meeting, he contrived to be alone in the house with me, and by blows—yes; blows and menaces, compelled me to submit to his ferocious desire; and, to avoid my mistress's fury, I was obliged in future to comply, and skulk to my loft at his command, in spite of increasing loathing.

"The anguish which was now pent up in my bosom, seemed to open a new world to me: I began to extend my thoughts beyond myself, and grieve for human misery, till I discovered, with horror—ah! what horror!—that I was with child. I know not why I felt a mixed sensation of despair and tenderness, excepting that, ever called a bastard, a bastard appeared to me an object of the greatest compassion in creation.

"I communicated this dreadful circumstance to my master, who was almost equally alarmed at the intelligence; for he feared his wife, and public censure at the meeting. After some weeks of deliberation had elapsed, I in continual fear that my altered shape would be noticed, my master gave me a medicine in a phial, which he desired me to take, telling me, without any circumlocution, for what purpose it was designed. I burst into tears, I thought it was killing myself—yet was such a self as I worth preserving? He cursed me for a fool, and left me to my own reflections. I could not resolve to take this infernal potion; but I wrapped it up in an old gown, and hid it in a corner of my box.

"Nobody yet suspected me, because they had been accustomed to view me as a creature of another species. But the threatening storm at last broke over my devoted head—never shall I forget it! One Sunday evening when I was left, as usual, to take care of the house, my master came home intoxicated, and I became the prey of his brutal appetite. His extreme intoxication made him forget his customary caution, and my mistress entered and found us in a situation that could not have been more hateful to her than me. Her husband was 'pot-valiant,' he feared her not at the moment, nor had he then much reason, for she instantly turned the whole force of her anger another way. She tore off my cap, scratched, kicked, and buffetted me, till she had exhausted her strength, declaring, as she rested her arm, 'that I had wheedled her husband from her.—But, could any thing better be expected from a wretch, whom she had taken into her house out of pure charity?' What a torrent of abuse rushed out? till, almost breathless, she concluded with saying, 'that I was born a strumpet; it ran in my blood, and nothing good could come to those who harboured me.'

"My situation was, of course, discovered, and she declared that I should not stay another night under the same roof with an honest family. I was therefore pushed out of doors, and my trumpery thrown after me, when it had been contemptuously examined in the passage, lest I should have stolen any thing.

"Behold me then in the street, utterly destitute! Whither could I creep for shelter? To my father's roof I had no claim, when not pursued by shame—now I shrunk back as from death, from my mother's cruel reproaches, my father's execrations. I could not endure to hear him curse the day I was born, though life had been a curse to me. Of death I thought, but with a confused emotion of terror, as I stood leaning my head on a post, and starting at every footstep, lest it should be my mistress coming to tear my heart out. One of the boys of the shop passing by, heard my tale, and immediately repaired to his master, to give him a description of my situation; and he touched the right key—the scandal it would give rise to, if I were left to repeat my tale to every enquirer. This plea came home to his reason, who had been sobered by his wife's rage, the fury of which fell on him when I was out of her reach, and he sent the boy to me with half-a-guinea, desiring him to conduct me to a house, where beggars, and other wretches, the refuse of society, nightly lodged.

"This night was spent in a state of stupefaction, or desperation. I detested mankind, and abhorred myself.

"In the morning I ventured out, to throw myself in my master's way, at his usual hour of going abroad. I approached him, he 'damned me for a b——, declared I had disturbed the peace of the family, and that he had sworn to his wife, never to take any more notice of me.' He left me; but, instantly returning, he told me that he should speak to his friend, a parish-offficer, to get a nurse for the brat I laid to him; and advised me, if I wished to keep out of the house of correction, not to make free with his name.

"I hurried back to my hole, and, rage giving place to despair, sought for the potion that was to procure abortion, and swallowed it, with a wish that it might destroy me, at the same time that it stopped the sensations of new-born life, which I felt with indescribable emotion. My head turned round, my heart grew sick, and in the horrors of approaching dissolution, mental anguish was swallowed up. The effect of the medicine was violent, and I was confined to my bed several days; but, youth and a strong constitution prevailing, I once more crawled out, to ask myself the cruel question, 'Whither I should go?' I had but two shillings left in my pocket, the rest had been expended, by a poor woman who slept in the same room, to pay for my lodging, and purchase the necessaries of which she partook.

"With this wretch I went into the neighbouring streets to beg, and my disconsolate appearance drew a few pence from the idle, enabling me still to command a bed; till, recovering from my illness, and taught to put on my rags to the best advantage, I was accosted from different motives, and yielded to the desire of the brutes I met, with the same detestation that I had felt for my still more brutal master. I have since read in novels of the blandishments of seduction, but I had not even the pleasure of being enticed into vice.

"I shall not," interrupted Jemima, "lead your imagination into all the scenes of wretchedness and depravity, which I was condemned to view; or mark the different stages of my debasing misery. Fate dragged me through the very kennels of society: I was still a slave, a bastard, a common property. Become familiar with vice, for I wish to conceal nothing from you, I picked the pockets of the drunkards who abused me; and proved by my conduct, that I deserved the epithets, with which they loaded me at moments when distrust ought to cease.

"Detesting my nightly occupation, though valuing, if I may

so use the word, my independence, which only consisted in choosing the street in which I should wander, or the roof, when I had money, in which I should hide my head, I was some time before I could prevail on myself to accept of a place in a house of ill fame, to which a girl, with whom I had accidentally conversed in the street, had recommended me. I had been hunted almost into a fever, by the watchmen of the quarter of the town I frequented; one, whom I had unwittingly offended, giving the word to the whole pack. You can scarcely conceive the tyranny exercised by these wretches: considering themselves as the instruments of the very laws they violate, the pretext which steels their conscience, hardens their heart. Not content with receiving from us, outlaws of society (let other women talk of favours) a brutal gratification gratuitously as a privilege of office, they extort a tithe of prostitution, and harrass with threats the poor creatures whose occupation affords not the means to silence the growl of avarice. To escape from this persecution, I once more entered into servitude.

"A life of comparative regularity restored my health; and— do not start—my manners were improved, in a situation where vice sought to render itself alluring, and taste was cultivated to fashion the person, if not to refine the mind. Besides, the common civility of speech, contrasted with the gross vulgarity to which I had been accustomed, was something like the polish of civilization. I was not shut out from all intercourse of humanity. Still I was galled by the yoke of service, and my mistress often flying into violent fits of passion, made me dread a sudden dismission, which I understood was always the case. I was therefore prevailed on, though I felt a horror of men, to accept the offer of a gentleman, rather in the decline of years, to keep his house, pleasantly situated in a little village near Hampstead.

"He was a man of great talents, and of brilliant wit; but, a worn-out votary of voluptuousness, his desires became fastidious in proportion as they grew weak, and the native tenderness of his heart was undermined by a vitiated imagination.

A thoughtless carreer of libertinism and social enjoyment, had injured his health to such a degree, that, whatever pleasure his conversation afforded me (and my esteem was ensured by proofs of the generous humanity of his disposition), the being his mistress was purchasing it at a very dear rate. With such a keen perception of the delicacies of sentiment, with an imagination invigorated by the exercise of genius, how could he sink into the grossness of sensuality!

"But, to pass over a subject which I recollect with pain, I must remark to you, as an answer to your often-repeated question, 'Why my sentiments and language were superior to my station?' that I now began to read, to beguile the tediousness of solitude, and to gratify an inquisitive, active mind. I had often, in my childhood, followed a ballad-singer, to hear the sequel of a dismal story, though sure of being severely punished for delaying to return with whatever I was sent to purchase. I could just spell and put a sentence together, and I listened to the various arguments, though often mingled with obscenity, which occurred at the table where I was allowed to preside: for a literary friend or two frequently came home with my master, to dine and pass the night. Having lost the privileged respect of my sex, my presence, instead of restraining, perhaps gave the reins to their tongues; still I had the advantage of hearing discussions, from which, in the common course of life, women are excluded.

"You may easily imagine, that it was only by degrees that I could comprehend some of the subjects they investigated, or acquire from their reasoning what might be termed a moral sense. But my fondness of reading increasing, and my master occasionally shutting himself up in this retreat, for weeks together, to write, I had many opportunities of improvement. At first, considering money (I was right!" exclaimed Jemima, altering her tone of voice) "as the only means, after my loss of reputation, of obtaining respect, or even the toleration of humanity, I had not the least scruple to secrete a part of the sums intrusted to me, and to screen myself from detection by a system of falshood. But, acquiring new principles, I began to have the ambition of returning to the respectable part of society, and was weak enough to suppose it possible. The attention of my unassuming instructor, who, without being ignorant of his own powers, possessed great simplicity of manners, strengthened the illusion. Having sometimes caught up hints for thought, from my untutored remarks, he often led me to discuss the subjects he was treating, and would read to me his productions, previous to their publication, wishing to profit by the criticism of unsophisticated feeling. The aim of his writings was to touch the simple springs of the heart; for he despised the would-be oracles, the self-elected philosophers, who fright away fancy, while sifting each grain of thought to prove that slowness of comprehension is wisdom.

"I should have distinguished this as a moment of sunshine, a happy period in my life, had not the repugnance the disgusting libertinism of my protector inspired, daily become more painful.—And, indeed, I soon did recollect it as such with agony, when his sudden death (for he had recourse to the most exhilarating cordials to keep up the convivial tone of his spirits) again threw me into the desert of human society. Had he had any time for reflection, I am certain he would have left the little property in his power to me: but, attacked by the fatal apoplexy in town, his heir, a man of rigid morals, brought his wife with him to take possession of the house and effects, before I was even informed of his death,—'to prevent,' as she took care indirectly to tell me, 'such a creature as she supposed me to be, from purloining any of them, had I been apprized of the event in time.'

"The grief I felt at the sudden shock the information gave me, which at first had nothing selfish in it, was treated with contempt, and I was ordered to pack up my clothes; and a few trinkets and books, given me by the generous deceased, were contested, while they piously hoped, with a reprobating shake of the head, 'that God would have mercy on his sinful soul!' With some difficulty, I obtained my arrears of wages; but asking—such is the spirit-grinding consequence of poverty and infamy—for a character for honesty and economy, which

God knows I merited, I was told by this—why must I call her woman?—'that it would go against her conscience to recommend a kept mistress.' Tears started in my eyes, burning tears; for there are situations in which a wretch is humbled by the contempt they are conscious they do not deserve.

"I returned to the metropolis; but the solitude of a poor lodging was inconceivably dreary, after the society I had enjoyed. To be cut off from human converse, now I had been taught to relish it, was to wander a ghost among the living. Besides, I foresaw, to aggravate the severity of my fate, that my little pittance would soon melt away. I endeavoured to obtain needlework; but, not having been taught early, and my hands being rendered clumsy by hard work, I did not sufficiently excel to be employed by the ready-made linen shops, when so many women, better qualified, were suing for it. The want of a character prevented my getting a place; for, irksome as servitude would have been to me, I should have made another trial, had it been feasible. Not that I disliked employment, but the inequality of condition to which I must have submitted. I had acquired a taste for literature, during the five years I had lived with a literary man, occasionally conversing with men of the first abilities of the age; and now to descend to the lowest vulgarity, was a degree of wretchedness not to be imagined unfelt. I had not, it is true, tasted the charms of affection, but I had been familiar with the graces of humanity.

"One of the gentlemen, whom I had frequently dined in company with, while I was treated like a companion, met me in the street, and enquired after my health. I seized the occasion, and began to describe my situation; but he was in haste to join, at dinner, a select party of choice spirits; therefore, without waiting to hear me, he impatiently put a guinea into my hand, saying, 'It was a pity such a sensible woman should be in distress—he wished me well from his soul.'

"To another I wrote, stating my case, and requesting advice. He was an advocate for unequivocal sincerity; and had often, in my presence, descanted on the evils which arise in society from the despotism of rank and riches.

"In reply, I received a long essay on the energy of the human mind, with continual allusions to his own force of character. He added, 'That the woman who could write such a letter as I had sent him, could never be in want of resources, were she to look into herself, and exert her powers; misery was the consequence of indolence, and, as to my being shut out from society, it was the lot of man to submit to certain privations.'

"How often have I heard," said Jemima, interrupting her narrative, "in conversation, and read in books, that every person willing to work may find employment? It is the vague assertion, I believe, of insensible indolence, when it relates to men; but, with respect to women, I am sure of its fallacy, unless they will submit to the most menial bodily labour; and even to be employed at hard labour is out of the reach of many, whose reputation misfortune or folly has tainted.

"How writers, professing to be friends to freedom, and the improvement of morals, can assert that poverty is no evil, I cannot imagine."

"No more can I," interrupted Maria, "yet they even expatiate on the peculiar happiness of indigence, though in what it can consist, excepting in brutal rest, when a man can barely earn a subsistence, I cannot imagine. The mind is necessarily imprisoned in its own little tenement; and, fully occupied by keeping it in repair, has not time to rove abroad for improvement. The book of knowledge is closely clasped, against those who must fulfil their daily task of severe manual labour or die; and curiosity, rarely excited by thought or information, seldom moves on the stagnate lake of ignorance."

"As far as I have been able to observe," replied Jemima, "prejudices, caught up by chance, are obstinately maintained by the poor, to the exclusion of improvement; they have not time to reason or reflect to any extent, or minds sufficiently exercised to adopt the principles of action, which form perhaps the only basis of contentment in every station."*

*The copy which appears to have received the author's last corrections, ends at this place. [Godwin's note]

"And independence," said Darnford, "they are necessarily strangers to, even the independence of despising their persecutors. If the poor are happy, or can be happy, *things are very well as they are.* And I cannot conceive on what principle those writers contend for a change of system, who support this opinion. The authors on the other side of the question are much more consistent, who grant the fact; yet, insisting that it is the lot of the majority to be oppressed in this life, kindly turn them over to another, to rectify the false weights and measures of this, as the only way to justify the dispensations of Providence. I have not," continued Darnford, "an opinion more firmly fixed by observation in my mind, than that, though riches may fail to produce proportionate happiness, poverty most commonly excludes it, by shutting up all the avenues to improvement."

"And as for the affections," added Maria, with a sigh, "how gross, and even tormenting do they become, unless regulated by an improving mind! The culture of the heart ever, I believe, keeps pace with that of the mind. But pray go on," addressing Jemima, "though your narrative gives rise to the most painful reflections on the present state of society."

"Not to trouble you," continued she, "with a detailed description of all the painful feelings of unavailing exertion, I have only to tell you, that at last I got recommended to wash in a few families, who did me the favour to admit me into their houses, without the most strict enquiry, to wash from one in the morning till eight at night, for eighteen or twenty-pence a day. On the happiness to be enjoyed over a washing-tub I need not comment; yet you will allow me to observe, that this was a wretchedness of situation peculiar to my sex. A man with half my industry, and, I may say, abilities, could have procured a decent livelihood, and discharged some of the duties which knit mankind together; whilst I, who had acquired a taste for the rational, nay, in honest pride let me assert it, the virtuous enjoyments of life, was cast aside as the filth of society. Condemned to labour, like a machine, only to earn bread, and scarcely that, I became melancholy and desperate.

"I have now to mention a circumstance which fills me with remorse, and fear it will entirely deprive me of your esteem. A tradesman became attached to me, and visited me frequently,—and I at last obtained such a power over him, that he offered to take me home to his house.—Consider, dear madam, I was famishing: wonder not that I became a wolf!—The only reason for not taking me home immediately, was the having a girl in the house, with child by him—and this girl—I advised him—yes, I did! would I could forget it!—to turn out of doors: and one night he determined to follow my advice. Poor wretch! She fell upon her knees, reminded him that he had promised to marry her, that her parents were honest!—What did it avail?—She was turned out.

"She approached her father's door, in the skirts of London, —listened at the shutters,—but could not knock. A watchman had observed her go and return several times—Poor wretch!—[The remorse Jemima spoke of, seemed to be stinging her to the soul, as she proceeded.]

"She left it, and, approaching a tub where horses were watered, she sat down in it, and, with desperate resolution, remained in that attitude—till resolution was no longer necessary!

"I happened that morning to be going out to wash, anticipating the moment when I should escape from such hard labour. I passed by, just as some men, going to work, drew out the stiff, cold corpse—Let me not recal the horrid moment!—I recognized her pale visage; I listened to the tale told by the spectators, and my heart did not burst. I thought of my own state, and wondered how I could be such a monster!—I worked hard; and, returning home, I was attacked by a fever. I suffered both in body and mind. I determined not to live with the wretch. But he did not try me; he left the neighbourhood. I once more returned to the wash-tub.

"Still this state, miserable as it was, admitted of aggravation. Lifting one day a heavy load, a tub fell against my shin, and gave me great pain. I did not pay much attention to the hurt, till it became a serious wound; being obliged to work as usual, or starve. But, finding myself at length unable to stand for any time, I thought of getting into an hospital. Hospitals, it should seem (for they are comfortless abodes for the sick) were expressly endowed for the reception of the friendless; yet I, who had on that plea a right to assistance, wanted the recommendation of the rich and respectable, and was several weeks languishing for admittance; fees were demanded on entering; and, what was still more unreasonable, security for burying me, that expence not coming into the letter of the charity. A guinea was the stipulated sum—I could as soon have raised a million; and I was afraid to apply to the parish for an order, lest they should have passed me, I knew not whither. The poor woman at whose house I lodged, compassionating my state, got me into the hospital; and the family where I received the hurt, sent me five shillings, three and six-pence of which I gave at my admittance—I know not for what.

"My leg grew quickly better; but I was dismissed before my cure was completed, because I could not afford to have my linen washed to appear decently, as the virago of a nurse said, when the gentlemen (the surgeons) came. I cannot give you an adequate idea of the wretchedness of an hospital; every thing is left to the care of people intent on gain. The attendants seem to have lost all feeling of compassion in the bustling discharge of their offices; death is so familiar to them, that they are not anxious to ward it off. Every thing appeared to be conducted for the accommodation of the medical men and their pupils, who came to make experiments on the poor, for the benefit of the rich. One of the physicians, I must not forget to mention, gave me half-a-crown, and ordered me some wine, when I was at the lowest ebb. I thought of making my case known to the lady-like matron; but her forbidding countenance prevented me. She condescended to look on the patients, and make general enquiries, two or three times a week; but the nurses knew the hour when the visit of ceremony would commence, and every thing was as it should be.

"After my dismission, I was more at a loss than ever for a subsistence, and, not to weary you with a repetition of the same unavailing attempts, unable to stand at the washing-tub, I began to consider the rich and poor as natural enemies, and became a thief from principle. I could not now cease to reason, but I hated mankind. I despised myself, yet I justified my conduct. I was taken, tried, and condemned to six months' imprisonment in a house of correction. My soul recoils with horror from the remembrance of the insults I had to endure, till, branded with shame, I was turned loose in the street, pennyless. I wandered from street to street, till, exhausted by hunger and fatigue, I sunk down senseless at a door, where I had vainly demanded a morsel of bread. I was sent by the inhabitant to the work-house, to which he had surlily bid me go, saying, he 'paid enough in conscience to the poor,' when, with parched tongue, I implored his charity. If those well-meaning people who exclaim against beggars, were acquainted with the treatment the poor receive in many of these wretched asylums, they would not stifle so easily involuntary sympathy, by saying that they have all parishes to go to, or wonder that the poor dread to enter the gloomy walls. What are the common run of workhouses, but prisons, in which many respectable old people, worn out by immoderate labour, sink into the grave in sorrow, to which they are carried like dogs!"

Alarmed by some indistinct noise, Jemima rose hastily to listen, and Maria, turning to Darnford, said, "I have indeed been shocked beyond expression when I have met a pauper's funeral. A coffin carried on the shoulders of three or four ill-looking wretches, whom the imagination might easily convert into a band of assassins, hastening to conceal the corpse, and quarrelling about the prey on their way. I know it is of little consequence how we are consigned to the earth; but I am led by this brutal insensibility, to what even the animal creation appears forcibly to feel, to advert to the wretched, deserted manner in which they died."

"True," rejoined Darnford, "and, till the rich will give more than a part of their wealth, till they will give time and attention to the wants of the distressed, never let them boast of charity. Let them open their hearts, and not their purses, and employ their minds in the service, if they are really actuated by humanity; or charitable institutions will always be the prey of the lowest order of knaves."

Jemima returning, seemed in haste to fiinish her tale. "The overseer farmed the poor of different parishes, and out of the bowels of poverty was wrung the money with which he purchased this dwelling, as a private receptacle for madness. He had been a keeper at a house of the same description, and conceived that he could make money much more readily in his old occupation. He is a shrewd—shall I say it?—villain. He observed something resolute in my manner, and offered to take me with him, and instruct me how to treat the disturbed minds he meant to intrust to my care. The offer of forty pounds a year, and to quit a workhouse, was not to be despised, though the condition of shutting my eyes and hardening my heart was annexed to it.

"I agreed to accompany him; and four years have I been attendant on many wretches, and"—she lowered her voice,— "the witness of many enormities. In solitude my mind seemed to recover its force, and many of the sentiments which I imbibed in the only tolerable period of my life, returned with their full force. Still what should induce me to be the champion for suffering humanity?—Who ever risked any thing for me?—Who ever acknowledged me to be a fellow-creature?"—

Maria took her hand, and Jemima, more overcome by kindness than she had ever been by cruelty, hastened out of the room to conceal her emotions.

Darnford soon after heard his summons, and, taking leave of him, Maria promised to gratify his curiosity, with respect to herself, the first opportunity.

CHAPTER 6

ACTIVE as love was in the heart of Maria, the story she had just heard made her thoughts take a wider range. The opening buds of hope closed, as if they had put forth too early, and the the happiest day of her life was overcast by the most melancholy reflections. Thinking of Jemima's peculiar fate and her own, she was led to consider the oppressed state of women, and to lament that she had given birth to a daughter. Sleep fled from her eyelids, while she dwelt on the wretchedness of unprotected infancy, till sympathy with Jemima changed to agony, when it seemed probable that her own babe might even now be in the very state she so forcibly described.

Maria thought, and thought again. Jemima's humanity had rather been benumbed than killed, by the keen frost she had to brave at her entrance into life; an appeal then to her feelings, on this tender point, surely would not be fruitless; and Maria began to anticipate the delight it would afford her to gain intelligence of her child. This project was now the only subject of reflection; and she watched impatiently for the dawn of day, with that determinate purpose which generally insures success.

At the usual hour, Jemima brought her breakfast, and a tender note from Darnford. She ran her eye hastily over it, and her heart calmly hoarded up the rapture a fresh assurance of affection, affection such as she wished to inspire, gave her, without diverting her mind a moment from its design. While Jemima waited to take away the breakfast, Maria alluded to the reflections, that had haunted her during the night to the exclusion of sleep. She spoke with energy of Jemima's unmerited sufferings, and of the fate of a number of deserted females, placed within the sweep of a whirlwind, from which it was next to impossible to escape. Perceiving the effect her conversation produced on the countenance of her guard, she grasped the arm of Jemima with that irresistible warmth which defies repulse, exclaiming—"With your heart, and such dreadful experience, can you lend your aid to deprive my babe of a mother's tenderness, a mother's care? In the name of God, assist me to snatch her from destruction! Let me but give her an education—let me but prepare her body and mind to encounter the ills which await her sex, and I will teach her to consider you as her second mother, and herself as the prop of your age. Yes, Jemima, look at me—observe me closely, and read my very soul; you merit a better fate;" she held out her hand with a firm gesture of assurance; "and I will procure it for you, as a testimony of my esteem, as well as of my gratitude."

Jemima had not power to resist this persuasive torrent; and, owning that the house in which she was confined, was situated on the banks of the Thames, only a few miles from London, and not on the sea-coast, as Darnford had supposed, she promised to invent some excuse for her absence, and go herself to trace the situation, and enquire concerning the health, of this abandoned daughter. Her manner implied an intention to do something more, but she seemed unwilling to impart her design; and Maria, glad to have obtained the main point, thought it best to leave her to the workings of her own mind; convinced that she had the power of interesting her still more in favour of herself and child, by a simple recital of facts.

In the evening, Jemima informed the impatient mother, that on the morrow she should hasten to town before the family hour of rising, and received all the information necessary, as a clue to her search. The "Good night!" Maria uttered was peculiarly solemn and affectionate. Glad expectation sparkled in her eye; and, for the first time since her detention, she pronounced the name of her child with pleasureable fondness; and, with all the garrulity of a nurse, described her first smile when she recognized her mother. Recollecting herself, a still kinder "Adieu!" with a "God bless you!"—that seemed to include a maternal benediction, dismissed Jemima.

The dreary solitude of the ensuing day, lengthened by impatiently dwelling on the same idea, was intolerably wearisome. She listened for the sound of a particular clock, which some directions of the wind allowed her to hear distinctly. She marked the shadow gaining on the wall; and, twilight thickening into darkness, her breath seemed oppressed while she anxiously counted nine.—The last sound was a stroke of despair on her heart; for she expected every moment, without seeing Jemima, to have her light extinguished by the savage female who supplied her place. She was even obliged to prepare for bed, restless as she was, not to disoblige her new attendant. She had been cautioned not to speak too freely to her; but the caution was needless, her countenance would still more emphatically have made her shrink back. Such was the ferocity of manner, conspicuous in every word and gesture of this hag, that Maria was afraid to enquire, why Jemima, who had faithfully promised to see her before her door was shut for the night, came not?—and, when the key turned in the lock, to consign her to a night of suspence, she felt a degree of anguish which the circumstances scarcely justified.

Continually on the watch, the shutting of a door, or the sound of a foot-step, made her start and tremble with apprehension, something like what she felt, when, at her entrance, dragged along the gallery, she began to doubt whether she were not surrounded by demons?

Fatigued by an endless rotation of thought and wild alarms, she looked like a spectre, when Jemima entered in the morning; especially as her eyes darted out of her head, to read in Jemima's countenance, almost as pallid, the intelligence she dared not trust her tongue to demand. Jemima put down the tea-things, and appeared very busy in arranging the table. Maria took up a cup with trembling hand, then forcibly recovering her fortitude, and restraining the convulsive movement which agitated the muscles of her mouth, she said, "Spare yourself the pain of preparing me for your information, I adjure you!—My child is dead!" Jemima solemnly answered, "Yes;" with a look expressive of compassion and angry emotions. "Leave me," added Maria, making a fresh effort to govern her feelings, and hiding her face in her handkerchief, to conceal her anguish—"It is enough—I know that my babe is no more—I will hear the particulars when I am"—*calmer*, she could not utter; and Jemima, without importuning her by idle attempts to console her, left the room.

Plunged in the deepest melancholy, she would not admit Darnford's visits; and such is the force of early associations even on strong minds, that, for a while, she indulged the superstitious notion that she was justly punished by the death of her child, for having for an instant ceased to regret her loss. Two or three letters from Darnford, full of soothing, manly tenderness, only added poignancy to these accusing emotions; yet the passionate style in which he expressed, what he termed the first and fondest wish of his heart, "that his affection might make her some amends for the cruelty and injustice she had endured," inspired a sentiment of gratitude to heaven; and her eyes filled with delicious tears, when, at the conclusion of his letter, wishing to supply the place of her unworthy relations, whose want of principle he execrated, he assured her, calling her his dearest girl, "that it should henceforth be the business of his life to make her happy."

He begged, in a note sent the following morning, to be permitted to see her, when his presence would be no intrusion on her grief; and so earnestly intreated to be allowed, according to promise, to beguile the tedious moments of absence, by dwelling on the events of her past life, that she sent him the memoirs which had been written for her daughter, promising Jemima the perusal as soon as he returned them.

CHAPTER 7

"ADDRESSING these memoirs to you, my child, uncertain whether I shall ever have an opportunity of instructing you, many observations will probably flow from my heart, which only a mother—a mother schooled in misery, could make.

"The tenderness of a father who knew the world, might be great; but could it equal that of a mother—of a mother, labouring under a portion of the misery, which the constitution of society seems to have entailed on all her kind? It is, my child, my dearest daughter, only such a mother, who will dare to break through all restraint to provide for your happiness— who will voluntarily brave censure herself, to ward off sorrow from your bosom. From my narrative, my dear girl, you may gather the instruction, the counsel, which is meant rather to exercise than influence your mind.—Death may snatch me from you, before you can weigh my advice, or enter into my reasoning: I would then, with fond anxiety, lead you very early in life to form your grand principle of action, to save you from the vain regret of having, through irresolution, let the spring-tide of existence pass away, unimproved, unenjoyed.— Gain experience—ah! gain it—while experience is worth having, and acquire sufficient fortitude to pursue your own happiness; it includes your utility, by a direct path. What is wisdom too often, but the owl of the goddess, who sits moping in a desolated heart; around me she shrieks, but I would invite all the gay warblers of spring to nestle in your blooming bosom. —Had I not wasted years in deliberating, after I ceased to doubt, how I ought to have acted—I might now be useful and happy.—For my sake, warned by my example, always appear what you are, and you will not pass through existence without enjoying its genuine blessings, love and respect.

"Born in one of the most romantic parts of England, an enthusiastic fondness for the varying charms of nature is the first sentiment I recollect; or rather it was the first consciousness of pleasure that employed and formed my imagination.

"My father had been a captain of a man of war; but, disgusted with the service, on account of the preferment of men whose chief merit was their family connections or borough interest, he retired into the country; and, not knowing what to do with himself—married. In his family, to regain his lost consequence, he determined to keep up the same passive obedience, as in the vessels in which he had commanded. His orders were not to be disputed; and the whole house was expected to fly, at the word of command, as if to man the shrouds, or mount aloft in an elemental strife, big with life or death. He was to be instantaneously obeyed, especially by my mother, whom he very benevolently married for love; but took care to remind her of the obligation, when she dared, in the slightest instance, to question his absolute authority. My eldest brother, it is true, as he grew up, was treated with more respect by my father; and became in due form the deputy-tyrant of the house. The representative of my father, a being privileged by nature—a boy, and the darling of my mother, he did not fail to act like an heir apparent. Such indeed was my mother's extravagant partiality, that, in comparison with her affection for him, she might be said not to love the rest of her children. Yet none of the children seemed to have so little affection for her. Extreme indulgence had rendered him so selfish, that he only thought of himself; and from tormenting insects and animals, he became the despot of his brothers, and still more of his sisters.

"It is perhaps difficult to give you an idea of the petty cares which obscured the morning of my life; continual restraint in the most trivial matters; unconditional submission to orders, which, as a mere child, I soon discovered to be unreasonable, because inconsistent and contradictory. Thus are we destined to experience a mixture of bitterness, with the recollection of our most innocent enjoyments.

"The circumstances which, during my childhood, occurred to fashion my mind, were various; yet, as it would probably afford me more pleasure to revive the fading remembrance of newborn delight, than you, my child, could feel in the perusal, I will not entice you to stray with me into the verdant meadow, to search for the flowers that youthful hopes scatter in every path; though, as I write, I almost scent the fresh green of spring—of that spring which never returns!

"I had two sisters, and one brother, younger than myself; my brother Robert was two years older, and might truly be termed the idol of his parents, and the torment of the rest of the family. Such indeed is the force of prejudice, that what was called spirit and wit in him, was cruelly repressed as forwardness in me.

"My mother had an indolence of character, which prevented her from paying much attention to our education. But the healthy breeze of a neighbouring heath, on which we bounded at pleasure, volatilized the humours that improper food might have generated. And to enjoy open air and freedom, was paradise, after the unnatural restraint of our fireside, where we were often obliged to sit three or four hours together, without daring to utter a word, when my father was out of humour, from want of employment, or of a variety of boisterous amusement. I had however one advantage, an instructor, the brother of my father, who, intended for the church, had of course received a liberal education. But, becoming attached to a young lady of great beauty and large fortune, and acquiring in the world some opinions not consonant with the profession for which he was designed, he accepted, with the most sanguine expectations of success, the offer of a nobleman to accompany him to India, as his confidential secretary.

"A correspondence was regularly kept up with the object of his affection; and the intricacies of business, peculiarly wearisome to a man of a romantic turn of mind, contributed, with a forced absence, to increase his attachment. Every other passion was lost in this master-one, and only served to swell the torrent. Her relations, such were his waking dreams, who had despised him, would court in their turn his alliance, and all the blandishments of taste would grace the triumph of love.—While he basked in the warm sunshine of love, friendship also promised to shed its dewy freshness; for a friend, whom he loved next to his mistress, was the confident, who forwarded the letters from one to the other, to elude the observation of prying relations. A friend false in similar circumstances, is, my dearest girl, an old tale; yet, let not this example, or the frigid caution of coldblooded moralists, make you endeavour to stifle hopes, which are the buds that naturally unfold themselves during the spring of life! Whilst your own heart is sincere, always expect to meet one glowing with the same sentiments; for to fly from pleasure, is not to avoid pain!

"My uncle realized, by good luck, rather than management, a handsome fortune; and returning on the wings of love, lost in the most enchanting reveries, to England, to share it with his mistress and his friend, he found them—united.

"There were some circumstances, not necessary for me to recite, which aggravated the guilt of the friend beyond measure, and the deception, that had been carried on to the last moment, was so base, it produced the most violent effect on my uncle's health and spirits. His native country, the world! lately a garden of blooming sweets, blasted by treachery, seemed changed into a parched desert, the abode of hissing serpents. Disappointment rankled in his heart; and, brooding over his wrongs, he was attacked by a raging fever, followed by a derangement of mind, which only gave place to habitual melancholy, as he recovered more strength of body.

"Declaring an intention never to marry, his relations were ever clustering about him, paying the grossest adulation to a man, who, disgusted with mankind, received them with scorn, or bitter sarcasms. Something in my countenance pleased him, when I began to prattle. Since his return, he appeared dead to affection; but I soon, by showing him innocent fondness, became a favourite; and endeavouring to enlarge and strengthen my mind, I grew dear to him in proportion as I imbibed his sentiments. He had a forcible manner of speaking, rendered more so by a certain impressive wildness of look and gesture, calculated to engage the attention of a young and ardent mind. It is not then surprising that I quickly adopted his opinions in preference, and reverenced him as one of a superior order of beings. He inculcated, with great warmth, self-respect, and a lofty consciousness of acting right, independent of the censure or applause of the world; nay, he almost taught me to brave, and even despise its censure, when convinced of the rectitude of my own intentions.

"Endeavouring to prove to me that nothing which deserved the name of love or friendship, existed in the world, he drew such animated pictures of his own feelings, rendered permanent by disappointment, as imprinted the sentiments strongly on my heart, and animated my imagination. These remarks are necessary to elucidate some peculiarities in my character, which by the world are indefinitely termed romantic.

"My uncle's increasing affection led him to visit me often. Still, unable to rest in any place, he did not remain long in the country to soften domestic tyranny; but he brought me books, for which I had a passion, and they conspired with his conversation, to make me form an ideal picture of life. I shall pass over the tyranny of my father, much as I suffered from it; but it is necessary to notice, that it undermined my mother's health; and that her temper, continually irritated by domestic bickering, became intolerably peevish.

"My eldest brother was articled to a neighbouring attorney, the shrewdest, and, I may add, the most unprincipled man in that part of the country. As my brother generally came home every Saturday, to astonish my mother by exhibiting his attainments, he gradually assumed a right of directing the whole family, not excepting my father. He seemed to take a peculiar pleasure in tormenting and humbling me; and if I ever ventured to complain of this treatment to either my father or mother, I was rudely rebuffed for presuming to judge of the conduct of my eldest brother.

"About this period a merchant's family came to settle in our neighbourhood. A mansion-house in the village, lately purchased, had been preparing the whole spring, and the sight of the costly furniture, sent from London, had excited my mother's envy, and roused my father's pride. My sensations were very different, and all of a pleasurable kind. I longed to see new characters, to break the tedious monotony of my life; and to find a friend, such as fancy had pourtrayed. I cannot then describe the emotion I felt, the Sunday they made their appearance at church. My eyes were rivetted on the pillar round which I expected first to catch a glimpse of them, and darted forth to meet a servant who hastily preceded a group of ladies, whose white robes and waving plumes, seemed to stream along the gloomy aisle, diffusing the light, by which I contemplated their figures.

"We visited them in form; and I quickly selected the eldest daughter for my friend. The second son, George, paid me particular attention, and finding his attainments and manners superior to those of the young men of the village, I began to imagine him superior to the rest of mankind. Had my home been more comfortable, or my previous acquaintance more numerous, I should not probably have been so eager to open my heart to new affections.

"Mr. Venables, the merchant, had acquired a large fortune by unremitting attention to business; but his health declining rapidly, he was obliged to retire, before his son, George, had acquired sufficient experience, to enable him to conduct their affairs on the same prudential plan, his father had invariably pursued. Indeed, he had laboured to throw off his authority, having despised his narrow plans and cautious speculation. The eldest son could not be prevailed on to enter the firm; and, to oblige his wife, and have peace in the house, Mr. Venables had purchased a commission for him in the guards.

"I am now alluding to circumstances which came to my knowledge long after; but it is necessary, my dearest child, that you should know the character of your father, to prevent your despising your mother; the only parent inclined to discharge a parent's duty. In London, George had acquired habits of libertinism, which he carefully concealed from his father and his commercial connections. The mask he wore, was so complete a covering of his real visage, that the praise his father lavished on his conduct, and, poor mistaken man! on his principles, contrasted with his brother's, rendered the notice he took of me peculiarly flattering. Without any fixed design, as I am now convinced, he continued to single me out at the dance, press my hand at parting, and utter expressions of unmeaning passion, to which I gave a meaning naturally suggested by the romantic turn of my thoughts. His stay in the country was short; his manners did not entirely please me; but, when he left us, the colouring of my picture became more vivid—Whither did not my imagination lead me? In short, I fancied myself in love—in love with the disinterestedness, fortitude, generosity, dignity, and humanity, with which I had invested the hero I dubbed. A circumstance which soon after occurred, rendered all these virtues palpable. [The incident is perhaps worth relating on other accounts, and therefore I shall describe it distinctly.]

"I had a great affection for my nurse, old Mary, for whom I used often to work, to spare her eyes. Mary had a younger sister, married to a sailor, while she was suckling me; for my mother only suckled my eldest brother, which might be the cause of her extraordinary partiality. Peggy, Mary's sister, lived with her, till her husband, becoming a mate in a West-Indian trader, got a little before-hand in the world. He wrote to his wife from the first port in the Channel, after his most successful voyage, to request her to come to London to meet him; he even wished her to determine on living there for the future, to save him the trouble of coming to her the moment he came on shore; and to turn a penny by keeping a green-stall. It was too much to set out on a journey the moment he had finished a voyage, and fifty miles by land, was worse than a thousand leagues by sea.

"She packed up her alls, and came to London—but did not meet honest Daniel. A common misfortune prevented her, and the poor are bound to suffer for the good of their country—he was pressed in the river—and never came on shore.

"Peggy was miserable in London, not knowing, as she said, 'the face of any living soul.' Besides, her imagination had been employed, anticipating a month or six weeks' happiness with her husband. Daniel was to have gone with her to Sadler's Wells, and Westminster Abbey, and to many sights, which he knew she never heard of in the country. Peggy too was thrifty, and how could she manage to put his plan in execution alone? He had acquaintance; but she did not know the very name of their places of abode. His letters were made up of—How do you does, and God bless yous,—information was reserved for the hour of meeting.

"She too had her portion of information, near at heart. Molly and Jacky were grown such little darlings, she was almost angry that daddy did not see their tricks. She had not half the pleasure she should have had from their prattle, could she have recounted to him each night the pretty speeches of the day. Some stories, however, were stored up—and Jacky could say papa with such a sweet voice, it must delight his heart. Yet when she came, and found no Daniel to greet her, when Jacky called papa, she wept, bidding 'God bless his innocent soul, that did not know what sorrow was.'—But more sorrow was in store for Peggy, innocent as she was.— Daniel was killed in the first engagement, and then the *papa* was agony, sounding to the heart.

"She had lived sparingly on his wages, while there was any hope of his return; but, that gone, she returned with a breaking heart to the country, to a little market town, nearly three miles from our village. She did not like to go to service, to be snubbed about, after being her own mistress. To put her children out to nurse was impossible: how far would her wages go? and to send them to her husband's parish, a distant one, was to lose her husband twice over.

"I had heard all from Mary, and made my uncle furnish a little cottage for her, to enable her to sell—so sacred was poor Daniel's advice, now he was dead and gone—a little fruit, toys and cakes. The minding of the shop did not require her whole time, nor even the keeping her children clean, and she loved to see them clean; so she took in washing, and altogether made a shift to earn bread for her children, still weeping for Daniel, when Jacky's arch looks made her think of his father. —It was pleasant to work for her children.—'Yes; from morning till night, could she have had a kiss from their father, God rest his soul! Yes; had it plased Providence to have let him come back without a leg or an arm, it would have been the same thing to her—for she did not love him because he maintained them—no; she had hands of her own.'

"The country people were honest, and Peggy left her linen out to dry very late. A recruiting party, as she supposed, passing through, made free with a large wash; for it was all swept away, including her own and her children's little stock.

"This was a dreadful blow; two dozen of shirts, stocks and handkerchiefs. She gave the money which she had laid by for half a year's rent, and promised to pay two shillings a week till all was cleared; so she did not lose her employment. This two shillings a week, and the buying a few necessaries for the children, drove her so hard, that she had not a penny to pay her rent with, when a twelvemonth's became due.

"She was now with Mary, and had just told her tale, which Mary instantly repeated—it was intended for my ear. Many houses in this town, producing a borough-interest, were included in the estate purchased by Mr. Venables, and the attorney with whom my brother lived, was appointed his agent, to collect and raise the rents.

"He demanded Peggy's, and, in spite of her intreaties, her poor goods had been seized and sold. So that she had not, and what was worse her children, 'for she had known sorrow enough,' a bed to lie on. She knew that I was good-natured—

right charitable, yet not liking to ask for more than needs must, she scorned to petition while people could any how be made to wait. But now, should she be turned out of doors, she must expect nothing less than to lose all her customers, and then she must beg or starve—and what would become of her children?—'had Daniel not been pressed—but God knows best—all this could not have happened.'

"I had two mattrasses on my bed; what did I want with two, when such a worthy creature must lie on the ground? My mother would be angry, but I could conceal it till my uncle came down; and then I would tell him all the whole truth, and if he absolved me, heaven would.

"I begged the house-maid to come up stairs with me (servants always feel for the distresses of poverty, and so would the rich if they knew what it was). She assisted me to tie up the mattrass; I discovering, at the same time, that one blanket would serve me till winter, could I persuade my sister, who slept with me, to keep my secret. She entering in the midst of the package, I gave her some new feathers, to silence her. We got the mattrass down the back stairs, unperceived, and I helped to carry it, taking with me all the money I had, and what I could borrow from my sister.

"When I got to the cottage, Peggy declared that she would not take what I had brought secretly; but, when, with all the eager eloquence inspired by a decided purpose, I grasped her hand with weeping eyes, assuring her that my uncle would screen me from blame, when he was once more in the country, describing, at the same time, what she would suffer in parting with her children, after keeping them so long from being thrown on the parish, she reluctantly consented.

"My project of usefulness ended not here; I determined to speak to the attorney; he frequently paid me compliments. His character did not intimidate me; but, imagining that Peggy must be mistaken, and that no man could turn a deaf ear to such a tale of complicated distress, I determined to walk to the town with Mary the next morning, and request him to wait for the rent, and keep my secret, till my uncle's return.

"My repose was sweet; and, waking with the first dawn of day, I bounded to Mary's cottage. What charms do not a light heart spread over nature! Every bird that twittered in a bush, every flower that enlivened the hedge, seemed placed there to awaken me to rapture—yes; to rapture. The present moment was full fraught with happiness; and on futurity I bestowed not a thought, excepting to anticipate my success with the attorney.

"This man of the world, with rosy face and simpering features, received me politely, nay kindly; listened with complacency to my remonstrances, though he scarcely heeded Mary's tears. I did not then suspect, that my eloquence was in my complexion, the blush of seventeen, or that, in a world where humanity to women is the characteristic of advancing civilization, the beauty of a young girl was so much more interesting than the distress of an old one. Pressing my hand, he promised to let Peggy remain in the house as long as I wished.—I more than returned the pressure—I was so grateful and so happy. Emboldened by my innocent warmth, he then kissed me— and I did not draw back—I took it for a kiss of charity.

"Gay as a lark, I went to dine at Mr. Venables'. I had previously obtained five shillings from my father, towards re-clothing the poor children of my care, and prevailed on my mother to take one of the girls into the house, whom I determined to teach to work and read.

"After dinner, when the younger part of the circle retired to the music room, I recounted with energy my tale; that is, I mentioned Peggy's distress, without hinting at the steps I had taken to relieve her. Miss Venables gave me half-a-crown; the heir five shillings; but George sat unmoved. I was cruelly distressed by the disappointment—I scarcely could remain on my chair; and, could I have got out of the room unperceived, I should have flown home, as if to run away from myself. After several vain attempts to rise, I leaned my head against the marble chimney-piece, and gazing on the evergreens that filled the fire-place, moralized on the vanity of human expec-

ations; regardless of the company. I was roused by a gentle
ap on my shoulder from behind Charlotte's chair. I turned
my head, and George slid a guinea into my hand, putting his
inger to his mouth, to enjoin me silence.

"What a revolution took place, not only in my train of
houghts, but feelings! I trembled with emotion—now, in-
leed, I was in love. Such delicacy too, to enhance his benevo-
ence! I felt in my pocket every five minutes, only to feel the
guinea; and its magic touch invested my hero with more than
mortal beauty. My fancy had found a basis to erect its model
of perfection on; and quickly went to work, with all the happy
credulity of youth, to consider that heart as devoted to virtue,
which had only obeyed a virtuous impulse. The bitter experience was yet to come, that has taught me how very distinct
are the principles of virtue, from the casual feelings from
which they germinate.

CHAPTER 8

"I HAVE perhaps dwelt too long on a circumstance, which is only of importance as it marks the progress of a deception that has been so fatal to my peace; and introduces to your notice a poor girl, whom, intending to serve, I led to ruin. Still it is probable that I was not entirely the victim of mistake; and that your father, gradually fashioned by the world, did not quickly become what I hesitate to call him—out of respect to my daughter.

"But, to hasten to the more busy scenes of my life. Mr. Venables and my mother died the same summer; and, wholly engrossed by my attention to her, I thought of little else. The neglect of her darling, my brother Robert, had a violent effect on her weakened mind; for, though boys may be reckoned the pillars of the house without doors, girls are often the only comfort within. They but too frequently waste their health and spirits attending a dying parent, who leaves them in comparative poverty. After closing, with filial piety, a father's eyes, they are chased from the paternal roof, to make room for the first-born, the son, who is to carry the empty family-name down to posterity; though, occupied with his own pleasures, he scarcely thought of discharging, in the decline of his parent's life, the debt contracted in his childhood. My mother's conduct led me to make these reflections. Great as was the fatigue I endured, and the affection my unceasing solicitude evinced, of which my mother seemed perfectly sensible, still, when my brother, whom I could hardly persuade to remain a quarter of an hour in her chamber, was with her alone, a short time before her death, she gave him a little hoard, which she had been some years accumulating.

"During my mother's illness, I was obliged to manage my father's temper, who, from the lingering nature of her malady, began to imagine that it was merely fancy. At this period, an artful kind of upper servant attracted my father's attention, and the neighbours made many remarks on the finery, not honestly got, exhibited at evening service. But I was too much occupied with my mother to observe any change in her dress or behaviour, or to listen to the whisper of scandal.

"I shall not dwell on the death-bed scene, lively as is the remembrance, or on the emotion produced by the last grasp of my mother's cold hand; when blessing me, she added, 'A little patience, and all will be over!' Ah! my child, how often have those words rung mournfully in my ears—and I have exclaimed—'A little more patience, and I too shall be at rest!'

"My father was violently affected by her death, recollected instances of his unkindness, and wept like a child.

"My mother had solemnly recommended my sisters to my care, and bid me be a mother to them. They, indeed, became more dear to me as they became more forlorn; for, during my mother's illness, I discovered the ruined state of my father's circumstances, and that he had only been able to keep up appearances, by the sums which he borrowed of my uncle.

"My father's grief, and consequent tenderness to his children, quickly abated, the house grew still more gloomy or riotous; and my refuge from care was again at Mr. Venables'; the young 'squire having taken his father's place, and allowing, for the present, his sister to preside at his table. George, though dissatisfied with his portion of the fortune, which had till lately been all in trade, visited the family as usual. He was now full of speculations in trade, and his brow became clouded by care. He seemed to relax in his attention to me, when the presence of my uncle gave a new turn to his behaviour. I was too unsuspecting, too disinterested, to trace these changes to their source.

My home every day became more and more disagreeable to me; my liberty was unnecessarily abridged, and my books, on the pretext that they made me idle, taken from me. My father's mistress was with child, and he, doating on her, allowed or overlooked her vulgar manner of tyrannizing over us. I was indignant, especially when I saw her endeavouring to attract, shall I say seduce? my younger brother. By allowing women but one way of rising in the world, the fostering the libertinism of men, society makes monsters of them, and then their ignoble vices are brought forward as a proof of inferiority of intellect.

The wearisomeness of my situation can scarcely be described. Though my life had not passed in the most even tenour with my mother, it was paradise to that I was destined to endure with my father's mistress, jealous of her illegitimate authority. My father's former occasional tenderness, in spite of his violence of temper, had been soothing to me; but now he only met me with reproofs or portentous frowns. The house-keeper, as she was now termed, was the vulgar despot of the family; and assuming the new character of a fine lady, she could never forgive the contempt which was sometimes visible in my countenance, when she uttered with pomposity her bad English, or affected to be well bred.

To my uncle I ventured to open my heart; and he, with his wonted benevolence, began to consider in what manner he could extricate me out of my present irksome situation. In spite of his own disappointment, or, most probably, actuated by the feelings that had been petrified, not cooled, in all their sanguine fervour, like a boiling torrent of lava suddenly dashing into the sea, he thought a marriage of mutual inclination (would envious stars permit it) the only chance for happiness in this disastrous world. George Venables had the reputation of being attentive to business, and my father's example gave great weight to this circumstance; for habits of order in business would, he conceived, extend to the regulation of the affections in domestic life. George seldom spoke in my uncle's company, except to utter a short, judicious question, or to make a pertinent remark, with all due deference to his superior judgment; so that my uncle seldom left his company without observing, that the young man had more in him than people supposed.

In this opinion he was not singular; yet, believe me, and I am not swayed by resentment, these speeches so justly poized, this silent deference, when the animal spirits of other young people were throwing off youthful ebullitions, were not the effect of thought or humility, but sheer barrenness of mind, and want of imagination. A colt of mettle will curvet and shew his paces. Yes; my dear girl, these prudent young men want all the fire necessary to ferment their faculties, and are characterized as wise, only because they are not foolish. It is true, that George was by no means so great a favourite of mine as during the first year of our acquaintance; still, as he often coincided in opinion with me, and echoed my sentiments; and having myself no other attachment, I heard with pleasure my uncle's proposal; but thought more of obtaining my freedom, than of my lover. But, when George, seemingly anxious for my happiness, pressed me to quit my present painful situation, my heart swelled with gratitude—I knew not that my uncle had promised him five thousand pounds.

Had this truly generous man mentioned his intention to me, I should have insisted on a thousand pounds being settled on each of my sisters; George would have contested; I should have seen his selfish soul; and—gracious God! have been spared the misery of discovering, when too late, that I was united to a heartless, unprincipled wretch. All my schemes of usefulness would not then have been blasted. The tenderness of my heart would not have heated my imagination with visions of the ineffable delight of happy love; nor would the sweet duty of a mother have been so cruelly interrupted.

But I must not suffer the fortitude I have so hardly acquired, to be undermined by unavailing regret. Let me hasten forward to describe the turbid stream in which I had to wade—but let me exultingly declare that it is passed—my soul holds fellowship with him no more. He cut the Gordian knot, which my principles, mistaken ones, respected; he dissolved the tie, the fetters rather, that ate into my very vitals—and I should rejoice, conscious that my mind is freed, though confined in hell itself; the only place that even fancy can imagine more dreadful than my present abode.

These varying emotions will not allow me to proceed. I heave sigh after sigh; yet my heart is still oppressed. For what am I reserved? Why was I not born a man, or why was I born at all?

CHAPTER 9

"I RESUME my pen to fly from thought. I was married; and we hastened to London. I had purposed taking one of my sisters with me; for a strong motive for marrying, was the desire of having a home at which I could receive them, now their own grew so uncomfortable, as not to deserve the cheering appellation. An objection was made to her accompanying me, that appeared plausible; and I reluctantly acquiesced. I was however willingly allowed to take with me Molly, poor Peggy's daughter. London and preferment, are ideas commonly associated in the country; and, as blooming as May, she bade adieu to Peggy with weeping eyes. I did not even feel hurt at the refusal in relation to my sister, till hearing what my uncle had done for me, I had the simplicity to request, speaking with warmth of their situation, that he would give them a thousand pounds a-piece, which seemed to me but justice. He asked me, giving me a kiss, 'If I had lost my senses?' I started back, as if I had found a wasp in a rose-bush. I expostulated. He sneered: and the demon of discord entered our paradise, to poison with his pestiferous breath every opening joy.

"I had sometimes observed defects in my husband's understanding; but, led astray by a prevailing opinion, that goodness of disposition is of the first importance in the relative situations of life, in proportion as I perceived the narrowness of his understanding, fancy enlarged the boundary of his heart. Fatal error! How quickly is the so much vaunted milkiness of nature turned into gall, by an intercourse with the world, if more generous juices do not sustain the vital source of virtue!

"One trait in my character was extreme credulity; but, when my eyes were once opened, I saw but too clearly all I had before overlooked. My husband was sunk in my esteem; still there are youthful emotions, which, for a while, fill up the chasm of love and friendship. Besides, it required some time to enable me to see his whole character in a just light, or rather to allow it to become fixed. While circumstances were ripening my faculties, and cultivating my taste, commerce and gross relaxations were shutting his against any possibility of improvement, till, by stifling every spark of virtue in himself, he began to imagine that it no where existed.

"Do not let me lead you astray, my child, I do not mean to assert, that any human being is entirely incapable of feeling the generous emotions, which are the foundation of every true principle of virtue; but they are frequently, I fear, so feeble, that, like the inflammable quality which more or less lurks in all bodies, they often lie for ever dormant; the circumstances never occurring, necessary to call them into action.

"I discovered however by chance, that, in consequence of some losses in trade, the natural effect of his gambling desire to start suddenly into riches, the five thousand pounds given me by my uncle, had been paid very opportunely. This discovery, strange as you may think the assertion, gave me pleasure; my husband's embarrassments endeared him to me. I was glad to find an excuse for his conduct to my sisters, and my mind became calmer.

"My uncle introduced me to some literary society; and the theatres were a never-failing source of amusement to me. My delighted eye followed Mrs. Siddons, when, with dignified delicacy, she played Califta; and I involuntarily repeated after her, in the same tone, and with a long-drawn sigh,

'Hearts like our's were pair'd—not match'd.'

"These were, at first, spontaneous emotions, though, becoming acquainted with men of wit and polished manners, I could not sometimes help regretting my early marriage; and that, in my haste to escape from a temporary dependence, and expand my newly fledged wings, in an unknown sky, I had been caught in a trap, and caged for life. Still the novelty of London, and the attentive fondness of my husband, for he had some personal regard for me, made several months glide away. Yet, not forgetting the situation of my sisters, who were still very young, I prevailed on my uncle to settle a thousand pounds on each; and to place them in a school near town, where I could frequently visit, as well as have them at home with me.

"I now tried to improve my husband's taste, but we had few subjects in common; indeed he soon appeared to have little relish for my society, unless he was hinting to me the use he could make of my uncle's wealth. When we had company, I was disgusted by an ostentatious display of riches, and I have often quitted the room, to avoid listening to exaggerated tales of money obtained by lucky hits.

"With all my attention and affectionate interest, I perceived that I could not become the friend or confident of my husband. Every thing I learned relative to his affairs I gathered up by accident; and I vainly endeavoured to establish, at our fire-side, that social converse, which often renders people of different characters dear to each other. Returning from the theatre, or any amusing party, I frequently began to relate what I had seen and highly relished; but with sullen taciturnity he soon silenced me. I seemed therefore gradually to lose, in his society, the soul, the energies of which had just been in action. To such a degree, in fact, did his cold, reserved manner affect me, that, after spending some days with him alone, I have imagined myself the most stupid creature in the world, till the abilities of some casual visitor convinced me that I had some dormant animation, and sentiments above the dust in which I had been groveling. The very countenance of my husband changed; his complexion became sallow, and all the charms of youth were vanishing with its vivacity.

"I give you one view of the subject; but these experiments and alterations took up the space of five years; during which period, I had most reluctantly extorted several sums from my

uncle, to save my husband, to use his own words, from destruction. At first it was to prevent bills being noted, to the
injury of his credit; then to bail him; and afterwards to prevent an execution from entering the house. I began at last to
conclude, that he would have made more exertions of his own
to extricate himself, had he not relied on mine, cruel as was
the task he imposed on me; and I firmly determined that I
would make use of no more pretexts.

"From the moment I pronounced this determination, indifference on his part was changed into rudeness, or something worse.

"He now seldom dined at home, and continually returned
at a late hour, drunk, to bed. I retired to another apartment;
I was glad, I own, to escape from his; for personal intimacy
without affection, seemed, to me the most degrading, as well
as the most painful state in which a woman of any taste, not
to speak of the peculiar delicacy of fostered sensibility, could
be placed. But my husband's fondness for women was of the
grossest kind, and imagination was so wholly out of the question, as to render his indulgences of this sort entirely promis-
cuous, and of the most brutal nature. My health suffered,
before my heart was entirely estranged by the loathsome
information; could I then have returned to his sullied arms,
but as a victim to the prejudices of mankind, who have made
women the property of their husbands? I discovered even, by
his conversation, when intoxicated that his favourites were
wantons of the lowest class, who could by their vulgar, inde-
cent mirth, which he called nature, rouse his sluggish spirits.
Meretricious ornaments and manners were necessary to attract his attention. He seldom looked twice at a modest
woman, and sat silent in their company; and the charms of
youth and beauty had not the slightest effect on his senses,
unless the possessors were initiated in vice. His intimacy with
profligate women, and his habits of thinking, gave him a contempt for female endowments; and he would repeat, when
wine had loosed his tongue, most of the common-place sarcasms levelled at them, by men who do not allow them to

have minds, because mind would be an impediment to gross enjoyment. Men who are inferior to their fellow men, are always most anxious to establish their superiority over women. But where are these reflections leading me?

"Women who have lost their husband's affection, are justly reproved for neglecting their persons, and not taking the same pains to keep, as to gain a heart; but who thinks of giving the same advice to men, though women are continually stigmatized for being attached to fops; and from the nature of their education, are more susceptible of disgust? Yet why a woman should be expected to endure a sloven, with more patience than a man, and magnanimously to govern herself, I cannot conceive; unless it be supposed arrogant in her to look for respect as well as a maintenance. It is not easy to be pleased, because, after promising to love, in different circumstances, we are told that it is our duty. I cannot, I am sure (though, when attending the sick, I never felt disgust) forget my own sensations, when rising with health and spirit, and after scenting the sweet morning, I have met my husband at the breakfast table. The active attention I had been giving to domestic regulations, which were generally settled before he rose, or a walk, gave a glow to my countenance, that contrasted with his squallid appearance. The squeamishness of stomach alone, produced by the last night's intemperance, which he took no pains to conceal, destroyed my appetite. I think I now see him lolling in an arm-chair, in a dirty powdering gown, soiled linen, ungartered stockings, and tangled hair, yawning and stretching himself. The newspaper was immediately called for, if not brought in on the tea-board, from which he would scarcely lift his eyes while I poured out the tea, excepting to ask for some brandy to put into it, or to declare that he could not eat. In answer to any question, in his best humour, it was a drawling 'What do you say, child?' But if I demanded money for the house expences, which I put off till the last moment, his customary reply, often prefaced with an oath, was, 'Do you think me, madam, made of money?'—The butcher, the baker, must wait; and, what was worse, I was often obliged to witness his surly dismission of tradesmen, who were in want of their money, and whom I sometimes paid with the presents my uncle gave me for my own use.

At this juncture my father's mistress, by terrifying his conscience, prevailed on him to marry her; he was already become a methodist; and my brother, who now practised for himself, had discovered a flaw in the settlement made on my mother's children, which set it aside, and he allowed my father, whose distress made him submit to any thing, a tithe of his own, or rather our fortune.

My sisters had left school, but were unable to endure home, which my father's wife rendered as disagreeable as possible, to get rid of girls whom she regarded as spies on her conduct. They were accomplished, yet you can (may you never be reduced to the same destitute state!) scarcely conceive the trouble I had to place them in the situation of governesses, the only one in which even a well-educated woman, with more than ordinary talents, can struggle for a subsistence; and even this is a dependence next to menial. Is it then surprising, that so many forlorn women, with human passions and feelings, take refuge in infamy? Alone in large mansions, I say alone, because they had no companions with whom they could converse on equal terms, or from whom they could expect the endearments of affection, they grew melancholy, and the sound of joy made them sad; and the youngest, having a more delicate frame, fell into a decline. It was with great difficulty that I, who now almost supported the house by loans from my uncle, could prevail on the *master* of it, to allow her a room to die in. I watched her sick bed for some months, and then closed her eyes, gentle spirit! for ever. She was pretty, with very engaging manners; yet had never an opportunity to marry, excepting to a very old man. She had abilities sufficient to have shone in any profession, had there been any professions for women, though she shrunk at the name of milliner or mantua-maker as degrading to a gentlewoman. I would not term this feeling false pride to any one but you, my child, whom I fondly hope to see (yes; I will indulge the hope for a

moment!) possessed of that energy of character which gives
dignity to any station; and with that clear, firm spirit that will
enable you to choose a situation for yourself, or submit to be
classed in the lowest, if it be the only one in which you can
be the mistress of your own actions.

"Soon after the death of my sister, an incident occurred, to
prove to me that the heart of a libertine is dead to natural
affection; and to convince me, that the being who has appeared all tenderness, to gratify a selfish passion, is as regardless of the innocent fruit of it, as of the object, when the fit is
over. I had casually observed an old, meanlooking woman,
who called on my husband every two or three months to
receive some money. One day entering the passage of his
little counting-house, as she was going out, I heard her say,
'The child is very weak; she cannot live long, she will soon die
out of your way, so you need not grudge her a little physic.'

" 'So much the better,' he replied, 'and pray mind your own
business, good woman.'

"I was struck by his unfeeling, inhuman tone of voice, and
drew back, determined when the woman came again, to try
to speak to her, not out of curiosity, I had heard enough, but
with the hope of being useful to a poor, outcast girl.

"A month or two elapsed before I saw this woman again;
and then she had a child in her hand that tottered along,
scarcely able to sustain her own weight. They were going
away, to return at the hour Mr. Venables was expected; he
was now from home. I desired the woman to walk into the
parlour. She hesitated, yet obeyed. I assured her that I should
not mention to my husband (the word seemed to weigh on my
respiration), that I had seen her, or his child. The woman
stared at me with astonishment; and I turned my eyes on the
squalid object [that accompanied her.] She could hardly support herself, her complexion was sallow, and her eyes in-
flamed, with an indescribable look of cunning, mixed with the
wrinkles produced by the peevishness of pain.

"Poor child!' I exclaimed. 'Ah! you may well say poor child,'
replied the woman. 'I brought her here to see whether he

would have the heart to look at her, and not get some advice I do not know what they deserve who nursed her. Why, her legs bent under her like a bow when she came to me, and she has never been well since; but, if they were no better paid than I am, it is not to be wondered at, sure enough.'

"On further enquiry I was informed, that this miserable spectacle was the daughter of a servant, a country girl, who caught Mr. Venables' eye, and whom he seduced. On his marriage he sent her away, her situation being too visible. After her delivery, she was thrown on the town; and died in an hospital within the year. The babe was sent to a parish-nurse, and afterwards to this woman, who did not seem much better; but what was to be expected from such a close bargain? She was only paid three shillings a week for board and washing.

"The woman begged me to give her some old clothes for the child, assuring me, that she was almost afraid to ask master for money to buy even a pair of shoes.

"I grew sick at heart. And, fearing Mr. Venables might enter, and oblige me to express my abhorrence, I hastily enquired where she lived, promised to pay her two shillings a week more, and to call on her in a day or two; putting a trifle into her hand as a proof of my good intention.

"If the state of this child affected me, what were my feelings at a discovery I made respecting Peggy——?*

*The manuscript is imperfect here. An episode seems to have been intended, which was never committed to paper. EDITOR. [Godwin's note]

CHAPTER 10

MY FATHER'S situation was now so distressing, that I prevailed on my uncle to accompany me to visit him; and to lend
me his assistance, to prevent the whole property of the family
from becoming the prey of my brother's rapacity; for, to extricate himself out of present difficulties, my father was totally
regardless of futurity. I took down with me some presents for
my step-mother; it did not require an effort for me to treat her
with civility, or to forget the past.

"This was the first time I had visited my native village, since
my marriage. But with what different emotions did I return
from the busy world, with a heavy weight of experience be-
numbing my imagination, to scenes, that whispered recollec-
tions of joy and hope most eloquently to my heart! The first
scent of the wild flowers from the heath, thrilled through my
veins, awakening every sense to pleasure. The icy hand of
despair seemed to be removed from my bosom; and—forget-
ing my husband—the nurtured visions of a romantic mind,
bursting on me with all their original wildness and gay exu-
berance, were again hailed as sweet realities. I forgot, with
equal facility, that I ever felt sorrow, or knew care in the
country; while a transient rainbow stole athwart the cloudy
sky of despondency. The picturesque form of several favourite trees, and the porches of rude cottages, with their smiling
hedges, were recognized with the gladsome playfulness of
childish vivacity. I could have kissed the chickens that pecked
on the common; and longed to pat the cows, and frolic with
the dogs that sported on it. I gazed with delight on the wind-

mill, and thought it lucky that it should be in motion, at the moment I passed by; and entering the dear green lane, which led directly to the village, the sound of the well-known rookery gave that sentimental tinge to the varying sensations of my active soul, which only served to heighten the lustre of the luxuriant scenery. But, spying, as I advanced, the spire, peeping over the withered tops of the aged elms that composed the rookery, my thoughts flew immediately to the churchyard, and tears of affection, such was the effect of my imagination, bedewed my mother's grave! Sorrow gave place to devotional feelings. I wandered through the church in fancy, as I used sometimes to do on a Saturday evening. I recollected with what fervour I addressed the God of my youth: and once more with rapturous love looked above my sorrows to the Father of nature. I pause——feeling forcibly all the emotions I am describing; and (reminded, as I register my sorrows, of the sublime calm I have felt, when in some tremendous solitude, my soul rested on itself, and seemed to fill the universe) I insensibly breathe soft, hushing every wayward emotion, as if fearing to sully with a sigh, a contentment so extatic.

"Having settled my father's affairs, and, by my exertions in his favour, made my brother my sworn foe, I returned to London. My husband's conduct was now changed; I had during my absence, received several affectionate, penitential letters from him; and he seemed on my arrival, to wish by his behaviour to prove his sincerity. I could not then conceive why he acted thus; and, when the suspicion darted into my head, that it might arise from observing my increasing influence with my uncle, I almost despised myself for imagining that such a degree of debasing selfishness could exist.

"He became, unaccountable as was the change, tender and attentive; and, attacking my weak side, made a confession of his follies, and lamented the embarrassments in which I, who merited a far different fate, might be involved. He besought me to aid him with my counsel, praised my understanding, and appealed to the tenderness of my heart.

"This conduct only inspired me with compassion. I wished

to be his friend; but love had spread his rosy pinions and fled far, far away; and had not (like some exquisite perfumes, the fine spirit of which is continually mingling with the air) left a fragrance behind, to mark where he had shook his wings. My husband's renewed caresses then became hateful to me; his brutality was tolerable, compared to his distasteful fondness. Still, compassion, and the fear of insulting his supposed feelings, by a want of sympathy, made me dissemble, and do violence to my delicacy. What a task!

"Those who support a system of what I term false refinement, and will not allow great part of love in the female, as well as male breast, to spring in some respects involuntarily, may not admit that charms are as necessary to feed the passion, as virtues to convert the mellowing spirit into friendship. To such observers I have nothing to say, any more than to the moralists, who insist that women ought to, and can love their husbands, because it is their duty. To you, my child, I may add, with a heart tremblingly alive to your future conduct, some observations, dictated by my present feelings, on calmly reviewing this period of my life. When novelists or moralists praise as a virtue, a woman's coldness of constitution, and want of passion; and make her yield to the ardour of her lover out of sheer compassion, or to promote a frigid plan of future comfort, I am disgusted. They may be good women, in the ordinary acceptation of the phrase, and do no harm; but they appear to me not to have those 'finely fashioned nerves,' which render the senses exquisite. They may possess tenderness; but they want that fire of the imagination, which produces *active* sensibility, and *positive* virtue. How does the woman deserve to be characterized, who marries one man, with a heart and imagination devoted to another? Is she not an object of pity or contempt, when thus sacrilegiously violating the purity of her own feelings? Nay, it is as indelicate, when she is indifferent, unless she be constitutionally insensible; then indeed it is a mere affair of barter; and I have nothing to do with the secrets of trade. Yes; eagerly as I wish you to possess true rectitude of mind, and purity of affection, I must insist that a heartless conduct is the contrary of virtuous. Truth is the only basis of virtue; and we cannot, without depraving our minds, endeavour to please a lover or husband, but in proportion as he pleases us. Men, more effectually to enslave us, may inculcate this partial morality, and lose sight of virtue in subdividing it into the duties of particular stations; but let us not blush for nature without a cause!

"After these remarks, I am ashamed to own, that I was pregnant. The greatest sacrifice of my principles in my whole life, was the allowing my husband again to be familiar with my person, though to this cruel act of self-denial, when I wished the earth to open and swallow me, you owe your birth; and I the unutterable pleasure of being a mother. There was something of delicacy in my husband's bridal attentions; but now his tainted breath, pimpled face, and blood-shot eyes, were not more repugnant to my senses, than his gross manners, and loveless familiarity to my taste.

"A man would only be expected to maintain; yes, barely grant a subsistence, to a woman rendered odious by habitual intoxication; but who would expect him, or think it possible to love her? And unless 'youth, and genial years were flown,' it would be thought equally unreasonable to insist, [under penalty of] forfeiting almost every thing reckoned valuable in life, that he should not love another: whilst woman, weak in reason, impotent in will, is required to moralize, sentimentalize herself to stone, and pine her life away, labouring to reform her embruted mate. He may even spend in dissipation, and intemperance, the very intemperance which renders him so hateful, her property, and by stinting her expences, not permit her to beguile in society, a wearisome, joyless life; for over their mutual fortune she has no power, it must all pass through his hand. And if she be a mother, and in the present state of women, it is a great misfortune to be prevented from discharging the duties, and cultivating the affections of one, what has she not to endure?——But I have suffered the tenderness of one to lead me into reflections that I did not think of making, to interrupt my narrative——yet the full heart will overflow.

"Mr. Venables' embarrassments did not now endear him to me; still, anxious to befriend him, I endeavoured to prevail on him to retrench his expences; but he had always some plausible excuse to give, to justify his not following my advice. Humanity, compassion, and the interest produced by a habit of living together, made me try to relieve, and sympathize with him; but, when I recollected that I was bound to live with such a being for ever—my heart died within me; my desire of improvement became languid, and baleful, corroding melancholy took possession of my soul. Marriage had bastilled me for life. I discovered in myself a capacity for the enjoyment of the various pleasures existence affords; yet, fettered by the partial laws of society, this fair globe was to me an universal blank.

"When I exhorted my husband to economy, I referred to himself. I was obliged to practise the most rigid, or contract debts, which I had too much reason to fear would never be paid. I despised this paltry privilege of a wife, which can only be of use to the vicious or inconsiderate, and determined not to increase the torrent that was bearing him down. I was then ignorant of the extent of his fraudulent speculations, whom I was bound to honour and obey.

"A woman neglected by her husband, or whose manners form a striking contrast with his, will always have men on the watch to soothe and flatter her. Besides, the forlorn state of a neglected woman, not destitute of personal charms, is particularly interesting, and rouses that species of pity, which is so near akin, it easily slides into love. A man of feeling thinks not of seducing, he is himself seduced by all the noblest emotions of his soul. He figures to himself all the sacrifices a woman of sensibility must make, and every situation in which his imagination places her, touches his heart, and fires his passions. Longing to take to his bosom the shorn lamb, and bid the drooping buds of hope revive, benevolence changes into passion: and should he then discover that he is beloved, honour binds him fast, though foreseeing that he may afterwards be obliged to pay severe damages to the man, who never appeared to value his wife's society, till he found that there was a chance of his being indemnified for the loss of it.

"Such are the partial laws enacted by men; for, only to lay a stress on the dependent state of a woman in the grand question of the comforts arising from the possession of property, she is [even in this article] much more injured by the loss of the husband's affection, than he by that of his wife; yet where is she, condemned to the solitude of a deserted home, to look for a compensation from the woman, who seduces him from her? She cannot drive an unfaithful husband from his house, nor separate, or tear, his children from him, however culpable he may be; and he, still the master of his own fate, enjoys the smiles of a world, that would brand her with infamy, did she, seeking consolation, venture to retaliate.

"These remarks are not dictated by experience; but merely by the compassion I feel for many amiable women, the *outlaws* of the world. For myself, never encouraging any of the advances that were made to me, my lovers dropped off like the untimely shoots of spring. I did not even coquet with them; because I found, on examining myself, I could not coquet with a man without loving him a little; and I perceived that I should not be able to stop at the line of what are termed *innocent freedoms*, did I suffer any. My reserve was then the consequence of delicacy. Freedom of conduct has emancipated many women's minds; but my conduct has most rigidly been governed by my principles, till the improvement of my understanding has enabled me to discern the fallacy of prejudices at war with nature and reason.

"Shortly after the change I have mentioned in my husband's conduct, my uncle was compelled by his declining health, to seek the succour of a milder climate, and embark for Lisbon. He left his will in the hands of a friend, an eminent solicitor; he had previously questioned me relative to my situation and state of mind, and declared very freely, that he could place no reliance on the stability of my husband's professions. He had been deceived in the unfolding of his character; he now thought it fixed in a train of actions that would inevitably lead to ruin and disgrace.

"The evening before his departure, which we spent alone together, he folded me to his heart, uttering the endearing appellation of 'child.'—My more than father! why was I not permitted to perform the last duties of one, and smooth the pillow of death? He seemed by his manner to be convinced that he should never see me more; yet requested me, most earnestly, to come to him, should I be obliged to leave my husband. He had before expressed his sorrow at hearing of my pregnancy, having determined to prevail on me to accompany him, till I informed him of that circumstance. He expressed himself unfeignedly sorry that any new tie should bind me to a man whom he thought so incapable of estimating my value; such was the kind language of affection.

"I must repeat his own words; they made an indelible impression on my mind:

" 'The marriage state is certainly that in which women, generally speaking, can be most useful; but I am far from thinking that a woman, once married, ought to consider the engagement as indissoluble (especially if there be no children to reward her for sacrificing her feelings) in case her husband merits neither her love, nor esteem. Esteem will often supply the place of love; and prevent a woman from being wretched, though it may not make her happy. The magnitude of a sacrifice ought always to bear some proportion to the utility in view; and for a woman to live with a man, for whom she can cherish neither affection nor esteem, or even be of any use to him, excepting in the light of a house-keeper, is an abjectness of condition, the enduring of which no concurrence of circumstances can ever make a duty in the sight of God or just men. If indeed she submits to it merely to be maintained in idleness, she has no right to complain bitterly of her fate; or to act, as a person of independent character might, as if she had a title to disregard general rules.

"But the misfortune is, that many women only submit in appearance, and forfeit their own respect to secure their reputation in the world. The situation of a woman separated from her husband, is undoubtedly very different from that of a man who has left his wife. He, with lordly dignity, has shaken of a clog; and the allowing her food and raiment, is thought sufficient to secure his reputation from taint. And, should she have been inconsiderate, he will be celebrated for his generosity and forbearance. Such is the respect paid to the master-key of property! A woman, on the contrary, resigning what is termed her natural protector (though he never was so, but in name) is despised and shunned, for asserting the independence of mind distinctive of a rational being, and spurning at slavery.'

"During the remainder of the evening, my uncle's tenderness led him frequently to revert to the subject, and utter, with increasing warmth, sentiments to the same purport. At length it was necessary to say 'Farewell!'—and we parted—gracious God! to meet no more.

CHAPTER 11

"A GENTLEMAN of large fortune and of polished manners, had lately visited very frequently at our house, and treated me, if possible, with more respect than Mr. Venables paid him; my pregnancy was not yet visible, his society was a great relief to me, as I had for some time past, to avoid expence, confined myself very much at home. I ever disdained unnecessary, perhaps even prudent concealments; and my husband, with great ease, discovered the amount of my uncle's parting present. A copy of a writ was the stale pretext to extort it from me; and I had soon reason to believe that it was fabricated for the purpose. I acknowledge my folly in thus suffering myself to be continually imposed on. I had adhered to my resolution not to apply to my uncle, on the part of my husband, any more; yet, when I had received a sum sufficient to supply my own wants, and to enable me to pursue a plan I had in view, to settle my younger brother in a respectable employment, I allowed myself to be duped by Mr. Venables' shallow pretences, and hypocritical professions.

"Thus did he pillage me and my family, thus frustrate all my plans of usefulness. Yet this was the man I was bound to respect and esteem: as if respect and esteem depended on an arbitrary will of our own! But a wife being as much a man's property as his horse, or his ass, she has nothing she can call her own. He may use any means to get at what the law considers as his, the moment his wife is in possession of it, even to the forcing of a lock, as Mr. Venables did, to search for notes in my writing-desk—and all this is done with a show of equity, because, forsooth, he is responsible for her maintenance.

"The tender mother cannot *lawfully* snatch from the gripe of the gambling spendthrift, or beastly drunkard, unmindful of his offspring, the fortune which falls to her by chance; or (so flagrant is the injustice) what she earns by her own exertions. No; he can rob her with impunity, even to waste publicly on a courtezan; and the laws of her country—if women have a country—afford her no protection or redress from the oppressor, unless she have the plea of bodily fear; yet how many ways are there of goading the soul almost to madness, equally unmanly, though not so mean? When such laws were framed, should not impartial lawgivers have first decreed, in the style of a great assembly, who recognized the existence of an *être suprême*, to fix the national belief, that the husband should always be wiser and more virtuous than his wife, in order to entitle him, with a show of justice, to keep this idiot, or perpetual minor, for ever in bondage. But I must have done —on this subject, my indignation continually runs away with me.

"The company of the gentleman I have already mentioned, who had a general acquaintance with literature and subjects of taste, was grateful to me; my countenance brightened up as he approached, and I unaffectedly expressed the pleasure I felt. The amusement his conversation afforded me, made it easy to comply with my husband's request, to endeavour to render our house agreeable to him.

"His attentions became more pointed; but, as I was not of the number of women, whose virtue, as it is termed, immediately takes alarm, I endeavoured, rather by raillery than serious expostulation, to give a different turn to his conversation. He assumed a new mode of attack, and I was, for a while, the dupe of his pretended friendship.

"I had, merely in the style of *badinage*, boasted of my conquest, and repeated his lover-like compliments to my husband. But he begged me, for God's sake, not to affront his friend, or I should destroy all his projects, and be his ruin. Had I had more affection for my husband, I should have expressed my contempt of this time-serving politeness:

now I imagined that I only felt pity; yet it would have puzzled a casuist to point out in what the exact difference consisted.

"This friend began now, in confidence, to discover to me the real state of my husband's affairs. 'Necessity,' said Mr. S——; why should I reveal his name? for he affected to palliate the conduct he could not excuse, 'had led him to take such steps, by accommodation bills, buying goods on credit, to sell them for ready money, and similar transactions, that his character in the commercial world was gone. He was considered,' he added, lowering his voice, 'on 'Change as a swindler.'

"I felt at that moment the first maternal pang. Aware of the evils my sex have to struggle with, I still wished, for my own consolation, to be the mother of a daughter; and I could not bear to think, that the *sins* of her father's entailed disgrace, should be added to the ills to which woman is heir.

"So completely was I deceived by these shows of friendship (nay, I believe, according to his interpretation, Mr. S—— really was my friend) that I began to consult him respecting the best mode of retrieving my husband's character: it is the good name of a woman only that sets to rise no more. I knew not that he had been drawn into a whirlpool, out of which he had not the energy to attempt to escape. He seemed indeed destitute of the power of employing his faculties in any regular pursuit. His principles of action were so loose, and his mind so uncultivated, that every thing like order appeared to him in the shape of restraint; and, like men in the savage state, he required the strong stimulus of hope or fear, produced by wild speculations, in which the interests of others went for nothing, to keep his spirits awake. He one time professed patriotism, but he knew not what it was to feel honest indignation; and pretended to be an advocate for liberty, when, with as little affection for the human race as for individuals, he thought of nothing but his own gratification. He was just such a citizen, as a father. The sums he adroitly obtained by a violation of the laws of his country, as well as those of humanity, he would allow a mistress to squander; though she was, with the same

sang froid, consigned, as were his children, to poverty, when
another proved more attractive.

"On various pretences, his friend continued to visit me;
and, observing my want of money, he tried to induce me to
accept of pecuniary aid; but this offer I absolutely rejected,
though it was made with such delicacy, I could not be dis-
pleased.

"One day he came, as I thought accidentally, to dinner. My
husband was very much engaged in business, and quitted the
room soon after the cloth was removed. We conversed as
usual, till confidential advice led again to love. I was extremely
mortified. I had a sincere regard for him, and hoped that he
had an equal friendship for me. I therefore began mildly to
expostulate with him. This gentleness he mistook for coy encouragement; and he would not be diverted from the subject.
Perceiving his mistake, I seriously asked him how, using such
language to me, he could profess to be my husband's friend?
A significant sneer excited my curiosity, and he, supposing
this to be my only scruple, took a letter deliberately out of his
pocket, saying, 'Your husband's honour is not inflexible. How
could you, with your discernment, think it so? Why, he left the
room this very day on purpose to give me an opportunity to
explain myself; *he* thought me too timid—too tardy.

"I snatched the letter with indescribable emotion. The purport of it was to invite him to dinner, and to ridicule his
chivalrous respect for me. He assured him, 'that every woman
had her price, and, with gross indecency, hinted, that he
should be glad to have the duty of a husband taken off his
hands. These he termed *liberal sentiments*. He advised him
not to shock my romantic notions, but to attack my credulous
generosity, and weak pity; and concluded with requesting
him to lend him five hundred pounds for a month or six
weeks.' I read this letter twice over; and the firm purpose it
inspired, calmed the rising tumult of my soul. I rose deliberately, requested Mr. S—— to wait a moment, and instantly
going into the counting-house, desired Mr. Venables to return
with me to the dining-parlour.

"He laid down his pen, and entered with me, without observing any change in my countenance. I shut the door, and, giving him the letter, simply asked, 'whether he wrote it, or was it a forgery?'

"Nothing could equal his confusion. His friend's eye met his, and he muttered something about a joke—But I interrupted him—'It is sufficient—We part for ever.'

"I continued, with solemnity, 'I have borne with your tyranny and infidelities. I disdain to utter what I have borne with. I thought you unprincipled, but not so decidedly vicious. I formed a tie, in the sight of heaven—I have held it sacred; even when men, more conformable to my taste, have made me feel—I despise all subterfuge!—that I was not dead to love. Neglected by you, I have resolutely stifled the enticing emotions, and respected the plighted faith you outraged. And you dare now to insult me, by selling me to prostitution!—Yes—equally lost to delicacy and principle—you dared sacrilegiously to barter the honour of the mother of your child.'

"Then, turning to Mr. S——, I added, 'I call on you, Sir, to witness,' and I lifted my hands and eyes to heaven, 'that, as solemnly as I took his name, I now abjure it,' I pulled off my ring, and put it on the table; 'and that I mean immediately to quit his house, never to enter it more. I will provide for myself and child. I leave him as free as I am determined to be myself —he shall be answerable for no debts of mine.'

"Astonishment closed their lips, till Mr. Venables, gently pushing his friend, with a forced smile, out of the room, nature for a moment prevailed, and, appearing like himself, he turned round, burning with rage, to me: but there was no terror in the frown, excepting when contrasted with the malignant smile which preceded it. He bade me 'leave the house at my peril; told me he despised my threats; I had no resource; I could not swear the peace against him!—I was not afraid of my life!—he had never struck me!'

"He threw the letter in the fire, which I had incautiously left in his hands; and, quitting the room, locked the door on me.

"When left alone, I was a moment or two before I could recollect myself—One scene had succeeded another with such rapidity, I almost doubted whether I was reflecting on a real event. 'Was it possible? Was I, indeed, free?'—Yes; free I termed myself, when I decidedly perceived the conduct I ought to adopt. How had I panted for liberty—liberty, that I would have purchased at any price, but that of my own esteem! I rose, and shook myself; opened the window, and methought the air never smelled so sweet. The face of heaven grew fairer as I viewed it, and the clouds seemed to flit away obedient to my wishes, to give my soul room to expand. I was all soul, and (wild as it may appear) felt as if I could have dissolved in the soft balmy gale that kissed my cheek, or have glided below the horizon on the glowing, descending beams. A seraphic satisfaction animated, without agitating my spirits; and my imagination collected, in visions sublimely terrible, or soothingly beautiful, an immense variety of the endless images, which nature affords, and fancy combines, of the grand and fair. The lustre of these bright picturesque sketches faded with the setting sun; but I was still alive to the calm delight they had diffused through my heart.

"There may be advocates for matrimonial obedience, who, making a distinction between the duty of a wife and of a human being, may blame my conduct.—To them I write not —my feelings are not for them to analyze; and may you, my child, never be able to ascertain, by heart-rending experience, what your mother felt before the present emancipation of her mind!

"I began to write a letter to my father, after closing one to my uncle; not to ask advice, but to signify my determination; when I was interrupted by the entrance of Mr. Venables. His manner was changed. His views on my uncle's fortune made him averse to my quitting his house, or he would, I am convinced, have been glad to have shaken off even the slight restraint my presence imposed on him; the restraint of showing me some respect. So far from having an affection for me, he really hated me, because he was convinced that I must despise him.

"He told me, that, 'As I now had had time to cool and reflect, he did not doubt but that my prudence, and nice sense of propriety, would lead me to overlook what was passed.'

" 'Reflection,' I replied, 'had only confirmed my purpose, and no power on earth could divert me from it.'

"Endeavouring to assume a soothing voice and look, when he would willingly have tortured me, to force me to feel his power, his countenance had an infernal expression, when he desired me, 'Not to expose myself to the servants, by obliging him to confine me in my apartment; if then I would give my promise not to quit the house precipitately, I should be free —and—.' I declared, interrupting him, 'that I would promise nothing. I had no measures to keep with him—I was resolved, and would not condescend to subterfuge.'

"He muttered, 'that I should soon repent of these preposterous airs;' and, ordering tea to be carried into my little study, which had a communication with my bed-chamber, he once more locked the door upon me, and left me to my own meditations. I had passively followed him up stairs, not wishing to fatigue myself with unavailing exertion.

"Nothing calms the mind like a fixed purpose. I felt as if I had heaved a thousand weight from my heart; the atmosphere seemed lightened; and, if I execrated the institutions of society, which thus enable men to tyrannize over women, it was almost a disinterested sentiment. I disregarded present inconveniences, when my mind had done struggling with itself,—when reason and inclination had shaken hands and were at peace. I had no longer the cruel task before me, in endless perspective, aye, during the tedious for ever of life, of labouring to overcome my repugnance—of labouring to extinguish the hopes, the maybes of a lively imagination. Death I had hailed as my only chance for deliverance; but, while existence had still so many charms, and life promised happiness, I shrunk from the icy arms of an unknown tyrant, though far more inviting than those of the man, to whom I supposed myself bound without any other alternative; and was content to linger a little longer, waiting for I knew not what, rather

than leave 'the warm precincts of the cheerful day,' and all
the unenjoyed affection of my nature.

"My present situation gave a new turn to my reflection; and
I wondered (now the film seemed to be withdrawn, that obscured the piercing sight of reason) how I could, previously to
the deciding outrage, have considered myself as everlastingly
united to vice and folly! 'Had an evil genius cast a spell at my
birth; or a demon stalked out of chaos, to perplex my understanding, and enchain my will, with delusive prejudices?'

"I pursued this train of thinking; it led me out of myself, to
expatiate on the misery peculiar to my sex. 'Are not,' I
thought, 'the despots for ever stigmatized, who, in the wan-
tonness of power, commanded even the most atrocious crimi-
nals to be chained to dead bodies? though surely those laws
are much more inhuman, which forge adamantine fetters to
bind minds together, that never can mingle in social com-
munion! What indeed can equal the wretchedness of that
state, in which there is no alternative, but to extinguish the
affections, or encounter infamy?'

CHAPTER 12

"Towards midnight Mr. Venables entered my chamber; and, with calm audacity preparing to go to bed, he bade me make haste, 'for that was the best place for husbands and wives to end their differences. He had been drinking plentifully to aid his courage.

"I did not at first deign to reply. But perceiving that he affected to take my silence for consent, I told him that, 'If he would not go to another bed, or allow me, I should sit up in my study all night.' He attempted to pull me into the chamber, half joking. But I resisted; and, as he had determined not to give me any reason for saying that he used violence, after a few more efforts, he retired, cursing my obstinacy, to bed.

"I sat musing some time longer; then, throwing my cloak around me, prepared for sleep on a sopha. And, so fortunate seemed my deliverance, so sacred the pleasure of being thus wrapped up in myself, that I slept profoundly, and woke with a mind composed to encounter the struggles of the day. Mr. Venables did not wake till some hours after; and then he came to me half-dressed, yawning and stretching, with haggard eyes, as if he scarcely recollected what had passed the preceding evening. He fixed his eyes on me for a moment, then, calling me a fool, asked 'How long I intended to continue this pretty farce? For his part, he was devilish sick of it; but this was the plague of marrying women who pretended to know something.'

"I made no other reply to this harangue, than to say, 'That he ought to be glad to get rid of a woman so unfit to be his companion—and that any change in my conduct would be mean dissimulation; for maturer reflection only gave the sacred seal of reason to my first resolution.'

"He looked as if he could have stamped with impatience, at being obliged to stifle his rage; but, conquering his anger (for weak people, whose passions seem the most ungovernable, restrain them with the greatest ease, when they have a sufficient motive), he exclaimed, 'Very pretty, upon my soul! very pretty, theatrical flourishes! Pray, fair Roxana, stoop from your altitudes, and remember that you are acting a part in real life.'

"He uttered this speech with a self-satisfied air, and went down stairs to dress.

"In about an hour he came to me again; and in the same tone said, 'That he came as my gentleman-usher to hand me down to breakfast.

" 'Of the black rod?' asked I.

"This question, and the tone in which I asked it, a little disconcerted him. To say the truth, I now felt no resentment; my firm resolution to free myself from my ignoble thraldom, had absorbed the various emotions which, during six years, had racked my soul. The duty pointed out by my principles seemed clear; and not one tender feeling intruded to make me swerve: The dislike which my husband had inspired was strong; but it only led me to wish to avoid, to wish to let him drop out of my memory; there was no misery, no torture that I would not deliberately have chosen, rather than renew my lease of servitude.

"During the breakfast, he attempted to reason with me on the folly of romantic sentiments; for this was the indiscriminate epithet he gave to every mode of conduct or thinking superior to his own. He asserted, 'that all the world were governed by their own interest; those who pretended to be actuated by different motives, were only deeper knaves, or fools crazed by books, who took for gospel all the rodomantade nonsense written by men who knew nothing of the world. For his part, he thanked God, he was no hypocrite; and,

if he stretched a point sometimes, it was always with an intention of paying every man his own.'

"He then artfully insinuated, 'that he daily expected a vessel to arrive, a successful speculation, that would make him
easy for the present, and that he had several other schemes
actually depending, that could not fail. He had no doubt of
becoming rich in a few years, though he had been thrown
back by some unlucky adventures at the setting out.'

"I mildly replied, 'That I wished he might not involve himself still deeper.'

"He had no notion that I was governed by a decision of
judgment, not to be compared with a mere spurt of resentment. He knew not what it was to feel indignation against
vice, and often boasted of his placable temper, and readiness
to forgive injuries. True; for he only considered the being
deceived, as an effort of skill he had not guarded against; and
then, with a cant of candour, would observe, 'that he did not
know how he might himself have been tempted to act in the
same circumstances.' And, as his heart never opened to
friendship, it never was wounded by disappointment. Every
new acquaintance he protested, it is true, was 'the cleverest
fellow in the world; and he really thought so; till the novelty
of his conversation or manners ceased to have any effect on
his sluggish spirits. His respect for rank or fortune was more
permanent, though he chanced to have no design of availing
himself of the influence of either to promote his own views.

"After a prefatory conversation,—my blood (I thought it
had been cooler) flushed over my whole countenance as he
spoke—he alluded to my situation. He desired me to reflect—'and act like a prudent woman, as the best proof of my
superior understanding; for he must own I had sense, did I
know how to use it. I was not,' he laid a stress on his words,
'without my passions; and a husband was a convenient cloke.
—He was liberal in his way of thinking; and why might not we,
like many other married people, who were above vulgar
prejudices, tacitly consent to let each other follow their own
inclination?—He meant nothing more, in the letter I made

the ground of complaint; and the pleasure which I seemed to take in Mr. S.'s company, led him to conclude, that he was not disagreeable to me.'

"A clerk brought in the letters of the day, and I, as I often did, while he was discussing subjects of business, went to the *piano forte*, and began to play a favourite air to restore myself, as it were, to nature, and drive the sophisticated sentiments I had just been obliged to listen to, out of my soul.

"They had excited sensations similar to those I have felt, in viewing the squalid inhabitants of some of the lanes and back streets of the metropolis, mortified at being compelled to consider them as my fellow-creatures, as if an ape had claimed kindred with me. Or, as when surrounded by a mephitical fog, I have wished to have a volley of cannon fired, to clear the incumbered atmosphere, and give me room to breathe and move.

"My spirits were all in arms, and I played a kind of extemporary prelude. The cadence was probably wild and impassioned, while, lost in thought, I made the sounds a kind of echo to my train of thinking.

"Pausing for a moment, I met Mr. Venables' eyes. He was observing me with an air of conceited satisfaction, as much as to say—'My last insinuation has done the business—she begins to know her own interest.' Then gathering up his letters, he said, 'That he hoped he should hear no more romantic stuff, well enough in a miss just come from boarding school;' and went, as was his custom, to the counting-house. I still continued playing; and, turning to a sprightly lesson, I executed it with uncommon vivacity. I heard footsteps approach the door, and was soon convinced that Mr. Venables was listening; the consciousness only gave more animation to my fingers. He went down into the kitchen, and the cook, probably by his desire, came to me, to know what I would please to order for dinner. Mr. Venables came into the parlour again, with apparent carelessness. I perceived that the cunning man was over-reaching himself; and I gave my directions as usual, and left the room.

"While I was making some alteration in my dress, Mr. Venables peeped in, and, begging my pardon for interrupting me, disappeared. I took up some work (I could not read), and two or three messages were sent to me, probably for no other purpose, but to enable Mr. Venables to ascertain what I was about.

"I listened whenever I heard the street-door open; at last I imagined I could distinguish Mr. Venables' step, going out. I laid aside my work; my heart palpitated; still I was afraid hastily to enquire; and I waited a long half hour, before I ventured to ask the boy whether his master was in the counting-house?

"Being answered in the negative, I bade him call me a coach, and collecting a few necessaries hastily together, with a little parcel of letters and papers which I had collected the preceding evening, I hurried into it, desiring the coachman to drive to a distant part of the town.

"I almost feared that the coach would break down before I got out of the street; and, when I turned the corner, I seemed to breathe a freer air. I was ready to imagine that I was rising above the thick atmosphere of earth; or I felt, as wearied souls might be supposed to feel on entering another state of existence.

"I stopped at one or two stands of coaches to elude pursuit, and then drove round the skirts of the town to seek for an obscure lodging, where I wished to remain concealed, till I could avail myself of my uncle's protection. I had resolved to assume my own name immediately, and openly to avow my determination, without any formal vindication, the moment I had found a home, in which I could rest free from the daily alarm of expecting to see Mr. Venables enter.

"I looked at several lodgings; but finding that I could not, without a reference to some acquaintance, who might inform my tyrant, get admittance into a decent apartment—men have not all this trouble—I thought of a woman whom I had assisted to furnish a little haberdasher's shop, and who I knew had a first floor to let.

"I went to her, and though I could not persuade her, that the quarrel between me and Mr. Venables would never be made up, still she agreed to conceal me for the present; yet assuring me at the same time, shaking her head, that, when a woman was once married, she must bear every thing. Her pale face, on which appeared a thousand haggard lines and delving wrinkles, produced by what is emphatically termed fretting, inforced her remark; and I had afterwards an opportunity of observing the treatment she had to endure, which grizzled her into patience. She toiled from morning till night; yet her husband would rob the till, and take away the money reserved for paying bills; and, returning home drunk, he would beat her if she chanced to offend him, though she had a child at the breast.

"These scenes awoke me at night; and, in the morning, I heard her, as usual, talk to her dear Johnny—he, forsooth, was her master; no slave in the West Indies had one more despotic; but fortunately she was of the true Russian breed of wives.

"My mind, during the few past days, seemed, as it were, disengaged from my body; but, now the struggle was over, I felt very forcibly the effect which perturbation of spirits produces on a woman in my situation.

"The apprehension of a miscarriage, obliged me to confine myself to my apartment near a fortnight; but I wrote to my uncle's friend for money, promising 'to call on him, and explain my situation, when I was well enough to go out; mean time I earnestly intreated him, not to mention my place of abode to any one, lest my husband—such the law considered him—should disturb the mind he could not conquer. I mentioned my intention of setting out for Lisbon, to claim my uncle's protection, the moment my health would permit.'

"The tranquillity however, which I was recovering, was soon interrupted. My landlady came up to me one day, with eyes swollen with weeping, unable to utter what she was commanded to say. She declared, 'That she was never so miserable in her life; that she must appear an ungrateful monster;

and that she would readily go down on her knees to me, to intreat me to forgive her, as she had done to her husband to spare her the cruel task.' Sobs prevented her from proceeding, or answering my impatient enquiries, to know what she meant.

"When she became a little more composed, she took a newspaper out of her pocket, declaring, 'that her heart smote her, but what could she do?—she must obey her husband.' I snatched the paper from her. An advertisement quickly met my eye, purporting, that 'Maria Venables had, without any assignable cause, absconded from her husband; and any person harbouring her, was menaced with the utmost severity of the law.'

"Perfectly acquainted with Mr. Venables' meanness of soul, this step did not excite my surprise, and scarcely my contempt. Resentment in my breast, never survived love. I bade the poor woman, in a kind tone, wipe her eyes, and request her husband to come up, and speak to me himself.

"My manner awed him. He respected a lady, though not a woman; and began to mutter out an apology.

" 'Mr. Venables was a rich gentleman; he wished to oblige me, but he had suffered enough by the law already, to tremble at the thought; besides, for certain, we should come together again, and then even I should not thank him for being accessary to keeping us asunder.—A husband and wife were, God knows, just as one,—and all would come round at last.' He uttered a drawling 'Hem!' and then with an arch look, added —'Master might have had his little frolics—but—Lord bless your heart!—men would be men while the world stands.'

"To argue with this privileged first-born of reason, I perceived, would be vain. I therefore only requested him to let me remain another day at his house, while I sought for a lodging; and not to inform Mr. Venables that I had ever been sheltered there.

"He consented, because he had not the courage to refuse a person for whom he had an habitual respect; but I heard the pent-up choler burst forth in curses, when he met his wife, who was waiting impatiently at the foot of the stairs, to know what effect my expostulations would have on him.

"Without wasting any time in the fruitless indulgence of vexation, I once more set out in search of an abode in which I could hide myself for a few weeks.

"Agreeing to pay an exorbitant price, I hired an apartment, without any reference being required relative to my character: indeed, a glance at my shape seemed to say, that my motive for concealment was sufficiently obvious. Thus was I obliged to shroud my head in infamy.

"To avoid all danger of detection—I use the appropriate word, my child, for I was hunted out like a felon—I determined to take possession of my new lodgings that very evening.

"I did not inform my landlady where I was going. I knew that she had a sincere affection for me, and would willingly have run any risk to show her gratitude; yet I was fully convinced, that a few kind words from Johnny would have found the woman in her, and her dear benefactress, as she termed me in an agony of tears, would have been sacrificed, to recompense her tyrant for condescending to treat her like an equal. He could be kind-hearted, as she expressed it, when he pleased. And this thawed sternness, contrasted with his habitual brutality, was the more acceptable, and could not be purchased at too dear a rate.

"The sight of the advertisement made me desirous of taking refuge with my uncle, let what would be the consequence; and I repaired in a hackney coach (afraid of meeting some person who might chance to know me, had I walked) to the chambers of my uncle's friend.

"He received me with great politeness (my uncle had already prepossessed him in my favour), and listened, with interest, to my explanation of the motives which had induced me to fly from home, and skulk in obscurity, with all the timidity of fear that ought only to be the companion of guilt. He lamented, with rather more gallantry than, in my situation, I thought delicate, that such a woman should be thrown away on a man insensible to the charms of beauty or grace. He seemed at a loss what to advise me to do, to evade my husband's search, without hastening to my uncle, whom, he hesitating said, I might not find alive. He uttered this intelligence with visible regret; requested me, at least, to wait for the arrival of the next packet; offered me what money I wanted, and promised to visit me.

"He kept his word; still no letter arrived to put an end to my painful state of suspense. I procured some books and music, to beguile the tedious solitary days.

> 'Come, ever smiling Liberty,
> 'And with thee bring thy jocund train:'

I sung—and sung till, saddened by the strain of joy, I bitterly lamented the fate that deprived me of all social pleasure. Comparative liberty indeed I had possessed myself of; but the jocund train lagged far behind!

CHAPTER 13

"BY WATCHING my only visitor, my uncle's friend, or by some other means, Mr. Venables discovered my residence, and came to enquire for me. The maid-servant assured him there was no such person in the house. A bustle ensued—I caught the alarm—listened—distinguished his voice, and immediately locked the door. They suddenly grew still; and I waited near a quarter of an hour, before I heard him open the parlour door, and mount the stairs with the mistress of the house, who obsequiously declared that she knew nothing of me.

"Finding my door locked, she requested me to 'open it, and prepare to go home with my husband, poor gentleman! to whom I had already occasioned sufficient vexation.' I made no reply. Mr. Venables then, in an assumed tone of softness, intreated me, 'to consider what he suffered, and my own reputation, and get the better of childish resentment.' He ran on in the same strain, pretending to address me, but evidently adapting his discourse to the capacity of the landlady; who, at every pause, uttered an exclamation of pity; or 'Yes, to be sure —Very true, sir.'

"Sick of the farce, and perceiving that I could not avoid the hated interview, I opened the door, and he entered. Advancing with easy assurance to take my hand, I shrunk from his touch, with an involuntary start, as I should have done from a noisome reptile, with more disgust than terror. His conductress was retiring, to give us, as she said, an opportunity to accommodate matters. But I bade her come in, or I would go out; and curiosity impelled her to obey me.

"Mr. Venables began to expostulate; and this woman, proud of his confidence, to second him. But I calmly silenced her, in the midst of a vulgar harangue, and turning to him, asked, 'Why he vainly tormented me? declaring that no power on earth should force me back to his house.'

"After a long altercation, the particulars of which, it would be to no purpose to repeat, he left the room. Some time was spent in loud conversation in the parlour below, and I discovered that he had brought his friend, an attorney, with him.†

The tumult on the landing place, brought out a gentleman, who had recently taken apartments in the house; he enquired why I was thus assailed?* The voluble attorney instantly repeated the trite tale. The stranger turned to me, observing, with the most soothing politeness and manly interest, that 'my countenance told a very different story.' He added, 'that I should not be insulted, or forced out of the house, by any body.'

" 'Not by her husband?' asked the attorney.

" 'No, sir, not by her husband.' Mr. Venables advanced towards him—But there was a decision in his attitude, that so well seconded that of his voice,‡ *   *   *   They left the house: at the same time protesting, that any one that should dare to protect me, should be prosecuted with the utmost rigour.

†In the original edition the paragraph following is preceded by three lines of asterisks [Publisher's note].

*The introduction of Darnford as the deliverer of Maria, in an early stage of the history, is already stated (Chap. III.) to have been an after-thought of the author. This has probably caused the imperfectness of the manuscript in the above passage; though, at the same time, it must be acknowledged to be somewhat uncertain, whether Darnford is the stranger intended in this place. It appears from Chap. XVII, that an interference of a more decisive nature was designed to be attributed to him. EDITOR. [Godwin's note]

‡Two and a half lines of asterisks appear here in the original [Publisher's note].

"They were scarcely out of the house, when my landlady came up to me again, and begged my pardon, in a very different tone. For, though Mr. Venables had bid her, at her peril, harbour me, he had not attended, I found, to her broad hints, to discharge the lodging. I instantly promised to pay her, and make her a present to compensate for my abrupt departure, if she would procure me another lodging, at a sufficient distance; and she, in return, repeating Mr. Venables' plausible tale, I raised her indignation, and excited her sympathy, by telling her briefly the truth.

"She expressed her commiseration with such honest warmth, that I felt soothed; for I have none of that fastidious sensitiveness, which a vulgar accent or gesture can alarm to the disregard of real kindness. I was ever glad to perceive in others the humane feelings I delighted to exercise; and the recollection of some ridiculous characteristic circumstances, which have occurred in a moment of emotion, has convulsed me with laughter, though at the instant I should have thought it sacrilegious to have smiled. Your improvement, my dearest girl, being ever present to me while I write, I note these feelings, because women, more accustomed to observe manners than actions, are too much alive to ridicule. So much so, that their boasted sensibility is often stifled by false delicacy. True sensibility, the sensibility which is the auxiliary of virtue, and the soul of genius, is in society so occupied with the feelings of others, as scarcely to regard its own sensations. With what reverence have I looked up at my uncle, the dear parent of my mind! when I have seen the sense of his own sufferings, of mind and body, absorbed in a desire to comfort those, whose misfortunes were comparatively trivial. He would have been ashamed of being as indulgent to himself, as he was to others. 'Genuine fortitude,' he would assert, 'consisted in governing our own emotions, and making allowance for the weaknesses in our friends, that we would not tolerate in ourselves.' But where is my fond regret leading me!

" 'Women must be submissive,' said my landlady. 'Indeed what could most women do? Who had they to maintain them, but their husbands? Every woman, and especially a lady, could not go through rough and smooth, as she had done, to earn a little bread.'

"She was in a talking mood, and proceeded to inform me how she had been used in the world. 'She knew what it was to have a bad husband, or she did not know who should.' I perceived that she would be very much mortified, were I not to attend to her tale, and I did not attempt to interrupt her, though I wished her, as soon as possible, to go out in search of a new abode for me, where I could once more hide my head.

"She began by telling me, 'That she had saved a little money in service; and was over-persuaded (we must all be in love once in our lives) to marry a likely man, a footman in the family, not worth a groat. My plan,' she continued, 'was to take a house, and let out lodgings; and all went on well, till my husband got acquainted with an impudent slut, who chose to live on other people's means—and then all went to rack and ruin. He ran in debt to buy her fine clothes, such clothes as I never thought of wearing myself, and—would you believe it? —he signed an execution on my very goods, bought with the money I worked so hard to get; and they came and took my bed from under me, before I heard a word of the matter. Aye, madam, these are misfortunes that you gentlefolks know nothing of,—but sorrow is sorrow, let it come which way it will.

"'I sought for a service again—very hard, after having a house of my own!—but he used to follow me, and kick up such a riot when he was drunk, that I could not keep a place; nay, he even stole my clothes, and pawned them; and when I went to the pawnbroker's, and offered to take my oath that they were not bought with a farthing of his money, they said, 'It was all as one, my husband had a right to whatever I had.'

"'At last he listed for a soldier, and I took a house, making an agreement to pay for the furniture by degrees; and I almost starved myself, till I once more got before-hand in the world.

"'After an absence of six years (God forgive me! I thought

he was dead) my husband returned; found me out, and came with such a penitent face, I forgave him, and clothed him from head to foot. But he had not been a week in the house, before some of his creditors arrested him; and, he selling my goods, I found myself once more reduced to beggary; for I was not as well able to work, go to bed late, and rise early, as when I quitted service; and then I thought it hard enough. He was soon tired of me, when there was nothing more to be had, and left me again.

"I will not tell you how I was buffeted about, till, hearing for certain that he had died in an hospital abroad, I once more returned to my old occupation; but have not yet been able to get my head above water: so, madam, you must not be angry if I am afraid to run any risk, when I know so well, that women have always the worst of it, when law is to decide.'

"After uttering a few more complaints, I prevailed on my landlady to go out in quest of a lodging; and, to be more secure, I condescended to the mean shift of changing my name.

"But why should I dwell on similar incidents!—I was hunted, like an infected beast, from three different apartments, and should not have been allowed to rest in any, had not Mr. Venables, informed of my uncle's dangerous state of health, been inspired with the fear of hurrying me out of the world as I advanced in my pregnancy, by thus tormenting and obliging me to take sudden journeys to avoid him; and then his speculations on my uncle's fortune must prove abortive.

"One day, when he had pursued me to an inn, I fainted, hurrying from him; and, falling down, the sight of my blood alarmed him, and obtained a respite for me. It is strange that he should have retained any hope, after observing my unwavering determination; but, from the mildness of my behaviour, when I found all my endeavours to change his disposition unavailing, he formed an erroneous opinion of my character, imagining that, were we once more together, I should part with the money he could not legally force from me, with the same facility as formerly. My forbearance and occasional sym-

pathy he had mistaken for weakness of character; and, because he perceived that I disliked resistance, he thought my
indulgence and compassion mere selfishness, and never discovered that the fear of being unjust, or of unnecessarily
wounding the feelings of another, was much more painful to
me, than any thing I could have to endure myself. Perhaps it
was pride which made me imagine, that I could bear what I
dreaded to inflict; and that it was often easier to suffer, than
to see the sufferings of others.

"I forgot to mention that, during this persecution, I received a letter from my uncle, informing me, 'that he only
found relief from continual change of air; and that he intended to return when the spring was a little more advanced
(it was now the middle of February), and then we would plan
a journey to Italy, leaving the fogs and cares of England far
behind.' He approved of my conduct, promised to adopt my
child, and seemed to have no doubt of obliging Mr. Venables
to hear reason. He wrote to his friend, by the same post,
desiring him to call on Mr. Venables in his name; and, in
consequence of the remonstrances he dictated, I was permitted to lie-in tranquilly.

"The two or three weeks previous, I had been allowed to
rest in peace; but, so accustomed was I to pursuit and alarm,
that I seldom closed my eyes without being haunted by Mr.
Venables' image, who seemed to assume terrific or hateful
forms to torment me, wherever I turned.—Sometimes a wild
cat, a roaring bull, or hideous assassin, whom I vainly attempted to fly; at others he was a demon, hurrying me to the
brink of a precipice, plunging me into dark waves, or horrid
gulfs; and I woke, in violent fits of trembling anxiety, to assure
myself that it was all a dream, and to endeavour to lure my
waking thoughts to wander to the delightful Italian vales, I
hoped soon to visit; or to picture some august ruins, where I
reclined in fancy on a mouldering column, and escaped, in the
contemplation of the heart-enlarging virtues of antiquity,
from the turmoil of cares that had depressed all the daring
purposes of my soul. But I was not long allowed to calm my

mind by the exercise of my imagination; for the third day after
your birth, my child, I was surprised by a visit from my elder
brother; who came in the most abrupt manner, to inform me
of the death of my uncle. He had left the greater part of his
fortune to my child, appointing me its guardian; in short,
every step was taken to enable me to be mistress of his fortune, without putting any part of it in Mr. Venables' power.
My brother came to vent his rage on me, for having, as he
expressed himself, 'deprived him, my uncle's eldest nephew,
of his inheritance;' though my uncle's property, the fruit of his
own exertion, being all in the funds, or on landed securities,
there was not a shadow of justice in the charge.

"As I sincerely loved my uncle, this intelligence brought on
a fever, which I struggled to conquer with all the energy of
my mind; for, in my desolate state, I had it very much at heart
to suckle you, my poor babe. You seemed my only tie to life,
a cherub, to whom I wished to be a father, as well as a mother;
and the double duty appeared to me to produce a proportionate increase of affection. But the pleasure I felt, while sustain-
ing you, snatched from the wreck of hope, was cruelly
damped by melancholy reflections on my widowed state—
widowed by the death of my uncle. Of Mr. Venables I thought
not, even when I thought of the felicity of loving your father,
and how a mother's pleasure might be exalted, and her care
softened by a husband's tenderness.—'Ought to be!' I exclaimed; and I endeavoured to drive away the tenderness that
suffocated me; but my spirits were weak, and the unbidden
tears would flow. 'Why was I,' I would ask thee, but thou didst
not heed me,—'cut off from the participation of the sweetest
pleasure of life?' I imagined with what extacy, after the pains
of child-bed, I should have presented my little stranger,
whom I had so long wished to view, to a respectable father,
and with what maternal fondness I should have pressed them
both to my heart!—Now I kissed her with less delight, though
with the most endearing compassion, poor helpless one! when
I perceived a slight resemblance of him, to whom she owed
her existence; or, if any gesture reminded me of him, even in

his best days, my heart heaved, and I pressed the innocent to my bosom, as if to purify it—yes, I blushed to think that its purity had been sullied, by allowing such a man to be its father.

"After my recovery, I began to think of taking a house in the country, or of making an excursion on the continent, to avoid Mr. Venables; and to open my heart to new pleasures and affection. The spring was melting into summer, and you, my little companion, began to smile—that smile made hope bud out afresh, assuring me the world was not a desert. Your gestures were ever present to my fancy; and I dwelt on the joy I should feel when you would begin to walk and lisp. Watching your wakening mind, and shielding from every rude blast my tender blossom, I recovered my spirits—I dreamed not of the frost—'the killing frost,' to which you were destined to be exposed.—But I lose all patience—and execrate the injustice of the world—folly! ignorance!—I should rather call it; but, shut up from a free circulation of thought, and always pondering on the same griefs, I writhe under the torturing apprehensions, which ought to excite only honest indignation, or active compassion; and would, could I view them as the natural consequence of things. But, born a woman—and born to suffer, in endeavouring to repress my own emotions, I feel more acutely the various ills my sex are fated to bear—I feel that the evils they are subject to endure, degrade them so far below their oppressors, as almost to justify their tyranny; leading at the same time superficial reasoners to term that weakness the cause, which is only the consequence of short-sighted despotism.

CHAPTER 14

"As MY MIND grew calmer, the visions of Italy again returned with their former glow of colouring; and I resolved on quitting the kingdom for a time, in search of the cheerfulness, that naturally results from a change of scene, unless we carry the barbed arrow with us, and only see what we feel.

"During the period necessary to prepare for a long absence, I sent a supply to pay my father's debts, and settled my brothers in eligible situations; but my attention was not wholly engrossed by my family, though I do not think it necessary to enumerate the common exertions of humanity. The manner in which my uncle's property was settled, prevented me from making the addition to the fortune of my surviving sister, that I could have wished; but I had prevailed on him to bequeath her two thousand pounds, and she determined to marry a lover, to whom she had been some time attached. Had it not been for this engagement, I should have invited her to accompany me in my tour; and I might have escaped the pit, so artfully dug in my path, when I was the least aware of danger.

"I had thought of remaining in England, till I weaned my child; but this state of freedom was too peaceful to last, and I had soon reason to wish to hasten my departure. A friend of Mr. Venables, the same attorney who had accompanied him in several excursions to hunt me from my hiding places, waited on me to propose a reconciliation. On my refusal, he indirectly advised me to make over to my husband—for husband he would term him—the greater part of the property I had at command, menacing me with continual persecution unless I complied, and that, as a last resort, he would claim the child. I did not, though intimidated by the last insinuation, scruple to declare, that I would not allow him to squander the money left to me for far different purposes, but offered him five hundred pounds, if he would sign a bond not to torment me any more. My maternal anxiety made me thus appear to waver from my first determination, and probably suggested to him, or his diabolical agent, the infernal plot, which has succeeded but too well.

"The bond was executed; still I was impatient to leave England. Mischief hung in the air when we breathed the same; I wanted seas to divide us, and waters to roll between, till he had forgotten that I had the means of helping him through a new scheme. Disturbed by the late occurrences, I instantly prepared for my departure. My only delay was waiting for a maid-servant, who spoke French fluently, and had been warmly recommended to me. A valet I was advised to hire, when I fixed on my place of residence for any time.

"My God, with what a light heart did I set out for Dover! —It was not my country, but my cares, that I was leaving behind. My heart seemed to bound with the wheels, or rather appeared the centre on which they twirled. I clasped you to my bosom, exclaiming 'And you will be safe—quite safe— when—we are once on board the packet.—Would we were there!' I smiled at my idle fears, as the natural effect of continual alarm; and I scarcely owned to myself that I dreaded Mr. Venables's cunning, or was conscious of the horrid delight he would feel, at forming stratagem after stratagem to circumvent me. I was already in the snare—I never reached the packet—I never saw thee more.—I grow breathless. I have scarcely patience to write down the details. The maid—the plausible woman I had hired—put, doubtless, some stupifying potion in what I ate or drank, the morning I left town. All I know is, that she must have quitted the chaise, shameless wretch! and taken (from my breast) my babe with her. How could a creature in a female form see me caress thee, and steal thee from my arms! I must stop, stop to repress a mother's anguish; lest, in bitterness of soul, I imprecate the wrath of heaven on this tiger, who tore my only comfort from me.

"How long I slept I know not; certainly many hours, for I woke at the close of day, in a strange confusion of thought. I was probably roused to recollection by some one thundering at a huge, unwieldy gate. Attempting to ask where I was, my voice died away, and I tried to raise it in vain, as I have done in a dream. I looked for my babe with affright; feared that it had fallen out of my lap, while I had so strangely forgotten her; and, such was the vague intoxication, I can give it no other name, in which I was plunged, I could not recollect when or where I last saw you; but I sighed, as if my heart wanted room to clear my head.

"The gates opened heavily, and the sullen sound of many locks and bolts drawn back, grated on my very soul, before I was appalled by the creeking of the dismal hinges, as they closed after me. The gloomy pile was before me, half in ruins; some of the aged trees of the avenue were cut down, and left to rot where they fell; and as we approached some mouldering steps, a monstrous dog darted forwards to the length of his chain, and barked and growled infernally.

"The door was opened slowly, and a murderous visage peeped out, with a lantern. 'Hush!' he uttered, in a threatning tone, and the affrighted animal stole back to his kennel. The door of the chaise flew back, the stranger put down the lantern, and clasped his dreadful arms around me. It was certainly the effect of the soporific draught, for, instead of exerting my strength, I sunk without motion, though not without sense, on his shoulder, my limbs refusing to obey my will. I was carried up the steps into a close-shut hall. A candle flaring in the socket, scarcely dispersed the darkness, though it displayed to me the ferocious countenance of the wretch who held me.

"He mounted a wide staircase. Large figures painted on the walls seemed to start on me, and glaring eyes to meet me at every turn. Entering a long gallery, a dismal shriek made me spring out of my conductor's arms, with I know not what mysterious emotion of terror; but I fell on the floor, unable to sustain myself.

"A strange-looking female started out of one of the recesses, and observed me with more curiosity than interest; till, sternly bid retire, she flitted back like a shadow. Other faces, strongly marked, or distorted, peeped through the half-opened doors, and I heard some incoherent sounds. I had no distinct idea where I could be—I looked on all sides, and almost doubted whether I was alive or dead.

"Thrown on a bed, I immediately sunk into insensibility again; and next day, gradually recovering the use of reason, I began, starting affrighted from the conviction, to discover where I was confined—I insisted on seeing the master of the mansion—I saw him—and perceived that I was buried alive.—

"Such, my child, are the events of thy mother's life to this dreadful moment—Should she ever escape from the fangs of her enemies, she will add the secrets of her prison-house—and—"

Some lines were here crossed out, and the memoirs broke off abruptly with the names of Jemima and Darnford.

APPENDIX

ADVERTISEMENT*

THE performance, with a fragment of which the reader has now been presented, was designed to consist of three parts. The preceding sheets were considered as constituting one of those parts. Those persons who in the perusal of the chapters, already written and in some degree finished by the author, have felt their hearts awakened, and their curiosity excited as to the sequel of the story, will, of course, gladly accept even of the broken paragraphs and half-finished sentences, which have been found committed to paper, as materials for the remainder. The fastidious and cold-hearted critic may perhaps feel himself repelled by the incoherent form in which they are presented. But an inquisitive temper willingly accepts the most imperfect and mutilated information, where better is not to be had: and readers, who in any degree resemble the author in her quick apprehension of sentiment, and of the pleasures and pains of imagination, will, I believe, find gratification, in contemplating sketches, which were designed in a short time to have received the finishing touches of her genius; but which must now for ever remain a mark to record the triumphs of mortality, over schemes of usefulness, and projects of public interest.

*Presumed to have been written by Godwin [Publisher's note].

CHAPTER 15

DARNFORD returned the memoirs to Maria, with a most affectionate letter, in which he reasoned on "the absurdity of the laws respecting matrimony, which, till divorces could be more easily obtained, was," he declared, "the most insufferable bondage. Ties of this nature could not bind minds governed by superior principles; and such beings were privileged to act above the dictates of laws they had no voice in framing, if they had sufficient strength of mind to endure the natural consequence. In her case, to talk of duty, was a farce, excepting what was due to herself. Delicacy, as well as reason, forbade her ever to think of returning to her husband: was she then to restrain her charming sensibility through mere prejudice? These arguments were not absolutely impartial, for he disdained to conceal, that, when he appealed to her reason, he felt that he had some interest in her heart.—The conviction was not more transporting, than sacred—a thousand times a day, he asked himself how he had merited such happiness?—and as often he determined to purify the heart she deigned to inhabit—He intreated to be again admitted to her presence."

He was; and the tear which glistened in his eye, when he respectfully pressed her to his bosom, rendered him peculiarly dear to the unfortunate mother. Grief had stilled the transports of love, only to render their mutual tenderness more touching. In former interviews, Darnford had contrived, by a hundred little pretexts, to sit near her, to take her hand, or to meet her eyes—now it was all soothing affection, and esteem seemed to have rivalled love. He adverted to her narrative, and spoke with warmth of the oppression she had endured.—His eyes, glowing with a lambent flame, told her how much he wished to restore her to liberty and love; but he kissed her hand, as if it had been that of a saint; and spoke of the loss of her child, as if it had been his own.—What could have been more flattering to Maria?—Every instance of self-denial was registered in her heart, and she loved him, for loving her too well to give way to the transports of passion.

They met again and again; and Darnford declared, while passion suffused his cheeks, that he never before knew what it was to love.—

One morning Jemima informed Maria, that her master intended to wait on her, and speak to her without witnesses. He came, and brought a letter with him, pretending that he was ignorant of its contents, though he insisted on having it returned to him. It was from the attorney already mentioned, who informed her of the death of her child, and hinted, "that she could not now have a legitimate heir, and that, would she make over the half of her fortune during life, she should be conveyed to Dover, and permitted to pursue her plan of travelling."

Maria answered with warmth, "That she had no terms to make with the murderer of her babe, nor would she purchase liberty at the price of her own respect."

She began to expostulate with her jailor; but he sternly bade her "Be silent—he had not gone so far, not to go further."

Darnford came in the evening. Jemima was obliged to be absent, and she, as usual, locked the door on them, to prevent interruption or discovery.—The lovers were, at first, embarrassed; but fell insensibly into confidential discourse. Darnford represented, "that they might soon be parted," and wished her "to put it out of the power of fate to separate them."

As her husband she now received him, and he solemnly pledged himself as her protector—and eternal friend.—

There was one peculiarity in Maria's mind: she was more

anxious not to deceive, than to guard against deception; and had rather trust without sufficient reason, than be for ever the prey of doubt. Besides, what are we, when the mind has, from reflection, a certain kind of elevation, which exalts the contemplation above the little concerns of prudence! We see what we wish, and make a world of our own—and, though reality may sometimes open a door to misery, yet the moments of happiness procured by the imagination, may, without a paradox, be reckoned among the solid comforts of life. Maria now, imagining that she had found a being of celestial mould—was happy,—nor was she deceived.—He was then plastic in her impassioned hand—and reflected all the sentiments which animated and warmed her.*

*Two and a half lines of dashes follow here in the original [Publisher's note].

CHAPTER 16

ONE morning confusion seemed to reign in the house, and Jemima came in terror, to inform Maria, "that her master had left it, with a determination, she was assured (and too many circumstances corroborated the opinion, to leave a doubt of its truth) of never returning. I am prepared then," said Jemima, "to accompany you in your flight."

Maria started up, her eyes darting towards the door, as if afraid that some one should fasten it on her for ever.

Jemima continued, "I have perhaps no right now to expect the performance of your promise; but on you it depends to reconcile me with the human race."

"But Darnford!"—exclaimed Maria, mournfully—sitting down again, and crossing her arms—"I have no child to go to, and liberty has lost its sweets."

"I am much mistaken, if Darnford is not the cause of my master's flight—his keepers assure me, that they have promised to confine him two days longer, and then he will be free —you cannot see him; but they will give a letter to him the moment he is free.—In that inform him where he may find you in London; fix on some hotel. Give me your clothes; I will send them out of the house with mine, and we will slip out at the garden-gate. Write your letter while I make these arrangements, but lose no time!"

In an agitation of spirit, not to be calmed, Maria began to write to Darnford. She called him by the sacred name of "husband," and bade him "hasten to her, to share her fortune, or she would return to him."—An hotel in the Adelphi was the place of rendezvous.

The letter was sealed and given in charge; and with light footsteps, yet terrified at the sound of them, she descended, scarcely breathing, and with an indistinct fear that she should never get out at the garden gate. Jemima went first.

A being, with a visage that would have suited one possessed by a devil, crossed the path, and seized Maria by the arm. Maria had no fear but of being detained—"Who are you? what are you?" for the form was scarcely human. "If you are made of flesh and blood," his ghastly eyes glared on her, "do not stop me!"

"Woman," interrupted a sepulchral voice, "what have I to do with thee?"—Still he grasped her hand, muttering a curse.

"No, no; you have nothing to do with me," she exclaimed, "this is a moment of life and death!"—

With supernatural force she broke from him, and, throwing her arms round Jemima, cried, "Save me!" The being, from whose grasp she had loosed herself, took up a stone as they opened the door, and with a kind of hellish sport threw it after them. They were out of his reach.

When Maria arrived in town, she drove to the hotel already fixed on. But she could not sit still—her child was ever before her; and all that had passed during her confinement, appeared to be a dream. She went to the house in the suburbs, where, as she now discovered, her babe had been sent. The moment she entered, her heart grew sick; but she wondered not that it had proved its grave. She made the necessary enquiries, and the church-yard was pointed out, in which it rested under a turf. A little frock which the nurse's child wore (Maria had made it herself) caught her eye. The nurse was glad to sell it for half-a-guinea, and Maria hastened away with the relic, and, reentering the hackney-coach which waited for her, gazed on it, till she reached her hotel.

She then waited on the attorney who had made her uncle's will, and explained to him her situation. He readily advanced her some of the money which still remained in his hands, and promised to take the whole of the case into consideration. Maria only wished to be permitted to remain in quiet—She found that several bills, apparently with her signature, had

been presented to her agent, nor was she for a moment at a
loss to guess by whom they had been forged; yet, equally
averse to threaten or intreat, she requested her friend [the
solicitor] to call on Mr. Venables. He was not to be found at
home; but at length his agent, the attorney, offered a condi-
tional promise to Maria, to leave her in peace, as long as she
behaved with propriety, if she would give up the notes. Maria
inconsiderately consented—Darnford was arrived, and she
wished to be only alive to love; she wished to forget the anguish she felt whenever she thought of her child.

They took a ready furnished lodging together, for she was
above disguise; Jemima insisting on being considered as her
house-keeper, and to receive the customary stipend. On no
other terms would she remain with her friend.

Darnford was indefatigable in tracing the mysterious circumstances of his confinement. The cause was simply, that a
relation, a very distant one, to whom he was heir, had died
intestate, leaving a considerable fortune. On the news of
Darnford's arrival [in England, a person, intrusted with the
management of the property, and who had the writings in his
possession, determining, by one bold stroke, to strip Darnford
of the succession,] had planned his confinement; and [as soon
as he had taken the measures he judged most conducive to his
object, this ruffian, together with his instrument,] the keeper
of the private mad-house, left the kingdom. Darnford, who
still pursued his enquiries, at last discovered that they had
fixed their place of refuge at Paris.

Maria and he determined therefore, with the faithful
Jemima, to visit that metropolis, and accordingly were preparing for the journey, when they were informed that Mr.
Venables had commenced an action against Darnford for seduction and adultery. The indignation Maria felt cannot be
explained; she repented of the forbearance she had exercised
in giving up the notes. Darnford could not put off his journey,
without risking the loss of his property: Maria therefore furnished him with money for his expedition; and determined to
remain in London till the termination of this affair.

She visited some ladies with whom she had formerly been intimate, but was refused admittance; and at the opera, or Ranelagh, they could not recollect her. Among these ladies there were some, not her most intimate acquaintance, who were generally supposed to avail themselves of the cloke of marriage, to conceal a mode of conduct, that would for ever have damned their fame, had they been innocent, seduced girls. These particularly stood aloof.—Had she remained with her husband, practicing insincerity, and neglecting her child to manage an intrigue, she would still have been visited and respected. If, instead of openly living with her lover, she could have condescended to call into play a thousand arts, which, degrading her own mind, might have allowed the people who were not deceived, to pretend to be so, she would have been caressed and treated like an honourable woman. "And Brutus* is an honourable man!" said Mark-Antony with equal sincerity.

With Darnford she did not taste uninterrupted felicity; there was a volatility in his manner which often distressed her; but love gladdened the scene; besides, he was the most tender, sympathizing creature in the world. A fondness for the sex often gives an appearance of humanity to the behaviour of men, who have small pretensions to the reality; and they seem to love others, when they are only pursuing their own gratification. Darnford appeared ever willing to avail himself of her taste and acquirements, while she endeavoured to profit by his decision of character, and to eradicate some of the romantic notions, which had taken root in her mind, while in adversity she had brooded over visions of unattainable bliss.

The real affections of life, when they are allowed to burst forth, are buds pregnant with joy and all the sweet emotions of the soul; yet they branch out with wild ease, unlike the artificial forms of felicity, sketched by an imagination painful alive. The substantial happiness, which enlarges and civilizes

*The name in the manuscript is by mistake written Caesar. EDITOR. [Godwin's note]

the mind, may be compared to the pleasure experienced in roving through nature at large, inhaling the sweet gale natural to the clime; while the reveries of a feverish imagination continually sport themselves in gardens full of aromatic shrubs, which cloy while they delight, and weaken the sense of pleasure they gratify. The heaven of fancy, below or beyond the stars, in this life, or in those ever-smiling regions surrounded by the unmarked ocean of futurity, have an insipid uniformity which palls. Poets have imagined scenes of bliss; but, sencing out sorrow, all the extatic emotions of the soul, and even its grandeur, seem to be equally excluded. We dose over the unruffled lake, and long to scale the rocks which fence the happy valley of contentment, though serpents hiss in the pathless desert, and danger lurks in the unexplored wiles. Maria found herself more indulgent as she was happier, and discovered virtues, in characters she had before disregarded, while chasing the phantoms of elegance and excellence, which sported in the meteors that exhale in the marshes of misfortune. The heart is often shut by romance against social pleasure; and, fostering a sickly sensibility, grows callous to the soft touches of humanity.

To part with Darnford was indeed cruel.—It was to feel most painfully alone; but she rejoiced to think, that she should spare him the care and perplexity of the suit, and meet him again, all his own. Marriage, as at present constituted, she considered as leading to immorality—yet, as the odium of society impedes usefulness, she wished to avow her affection to Darnford, by becoming his wife according to established rules; not to be confounded with women who act from very different motives, though her conduct would be just the same without the ceremony as with it, and her expectations from him not less firm. The being summoned to defend herself from a charge which she was determined to plead guilty to, was still galling, as it roused bitter reflections on the situation of women in society.

CHAPTER 17

SUCH was her state of mind when the dogs of law were let loose on her. Maria took the task of conducting Darnford's defence upon herself. She instructed his counsel to plead guilty to the charge of adultery; but to deny that of seduction.

The counsel for the plaintiff opened the cause, by observing, "that his client had ever been an indulgent husband, and had borne with several defects of temper, while he had nothing criminal to lay to the charge of his wife. But that she left his house without assigning any cause. He could not assert that she was then acquainted with the defendant; yet, when he was once endeavouring to bring her back to her home, this man put the peace-officers to flight, and took her he knew not whither. After the birth of her child, her conduct was so strange, and a melancholy malady having afflicted one of the family, which delicacy forbade the dwelling on, it was necessary to confine her. By some means the defendant enabled her to make her escape, and they had lived together, in despite of all sense of order and decorum. The adultery was allowed, it was not necessary to bring any witnesses to prove it; but the seduction, though highly probable from the circumstances which he had the honour to state, could not be so clearly proved.—It was of the most atrocious kind, as decency was set at defiance, and respect for reputation, which shows internal compunction, utterly disregarded."

A strong sense of injustice had silenced every motion, which a mixture of true and false delicacy might otherwise have excited in Maria's bosom. She only felt in earnest to insist on the privilege of her nature. The sarcasms of society, and the condemnations of a mistaken world, were nothing to her, compared with acting contrary to those feelings which were the foundation of her principles. [She therefore eagerly put herself forward, instead of desiring to be absent, on this memorable occasion.]

Convinced that the subterfuges of the law were disgraceful, she wrote a paper, which she expressly desired might be read in court:

"Married when scarcely able to distinguish the nature of the engagement, I yet submitted to the rigid laws which enslave women, and obeyed the man whom I could no longer love. Whether the duties of the state are reciprocal, I mean not to discuss; but I can prove repeated infidelities which I overlooked or pardoned. Witnesses are not wanting to establish these facts. I at present maintain the child of a maid servant, sworn to him, and born after our marriage. I am ready to allow, that education and circumstances lead men to think and act with less delicacy, than the preservation of order in society demands from women; but surely I may without assumption declare, that, though I could excuse the birth, I could not the desertion of this unfortunate babe:—and, while I despised the man, it was not easy to venerate the husband. With proper restrictions however, I revere the institution which fraternizes the world. I exclaim against the laws which throw the whole weight of the yoke on the weaker shoulders, and force women, when they claim protectorship as mothers, to sign a contract, which renders them dependent on the caprice of the tyrant, whom choice or necessity has appointed to reign over them. Various are the cases, in which a woman ought to separate herself from her husband; and mine, I may be allowed emphatically to insist, comes under the description of the most aggravated.

"I will not enlarge on those provocations which only the individual can estimate; but will bring forward such charges only, the truth of which is an insult upon humanity. In order to promote certain destructive speculations, Mr. Venables prevailed on me to borrow certain sums of a wealthy relation; and, when I refused further compliance, he thought of barter- ing my person; and not only allowed opportunities to, but urged, a friend from whom he borrowed money, to seduce me. On the discovery of this act of atrocity, I determined to leave him, and in the most decided manner, for ever. I con- sider all obligations as made void by his conduct; and hold, that schisms which proceed from want of principles, can never be healed.

"He received a fortune with me to the amount of five thou- sand pounds. On the death of my uncle, convinced that I could provide for my child, I destroyed the settlement of that fortune. I required none of my property to be returned to me, nor shall enumerate the sums extorted from me during six years that we lived together.

"After leaving, what the law considers as my home, I was hunted like a criminal from place to place, though I con- tracted no debts, and demanded no maintenance—yet, as the laws sanction such proceeding, and make women the prop- erty of their husbands, I forbear to animadvert. After the birth of my daughter, and the death of my uncle, who left a very considerable property to myself and child, I was exposed to new persecution; and, because I had, before arriving at what is termed years of discretion, pledged my faith, I was treated by the world, as bound for ever to a man whose vices were notorious. Yet what are the vices generally known, to the various miseries that a woman may be subject to, which, though deeply felt, eating into the soul, elude description, and may be glossed over! A false morality is even established, which makes all the virtue of women consist in chastity, sub- mission, and the forgiveness of injuries.

"I pardon my oppressor—bitterly as I lament the loss of my child, torn from me in the most violent manner. But nature revolts, and my soul sickens at the bare supposition, that it could ever be a duty to pretend affection, when a separation is necessary to prevent my feeling hourly aversion.

"To force me to give my fortune, I was imprisoned—yes; in

a private mad-house.—There, in the heart of misery, I met the man charged with seducing me. We became attached—I deemed, and ever shall deem, myself free. The death of my babe dissolved the only tie which subsisted between me and my, what is termed, lawful husband.

"To this person, thus encountered, I voluntarily gave myself, never considering myself as any more bound to transgress the laws of moral purity, because the will of my husband might be pleaded in my excuse, than to transgress those laws to which [the policy of artificial society has] annexed [positive] punishments.—While no command of a husband can prevent a woman from suffering for certain crimes, she must be allowed to consult her conscience, and regulate her conduct, in some degree, by her own sense of right. The respect I owe to myself, demanded my strict adherence to my determination of never viewing Mr. Venables in the light of a husband, nor could it forbid me from encouraging another. If I am unfortunately united to an unprincipled man, am I for ever to be shut out from fulfilling the duties of a wife and mother?—I wish my country to approve of my conduct; but, if laws exist, made by the strong to oppress the weak, I appeal to my own sense of justice, and declare that I will not live with the individual, who has violated every moral obligation which binds man to man.

"I protest equally against any charge being brought to criminate the man, whom I consider as my husband. I was six-and-twenty when I left Mr. Venables' roof; if ever I am to be supposed to arrive at an age to direct my own actions, I must by that time have arrived at it.—I acted with deliberation.—Mr. Darnford found me a forlorn and oppressed woman, and promised the protection women in the present state of society want.—But the man who now claims me—was he deprived of my society by this conduct? The question is an insult to common sense, considering where Mr. Darnford met me.—Mr. Venables' door was indeed open to me—nay, threats and intreaties were used to induce me to return; but why? Was affection or honour the motive?—I cannot, it is true, dive into the recesses of the human heart—yet I presume to assert, [borne out as I am by a variety of circumstances,] that he was merely influenced by the most rapacious avarice.

"I claim then a divorce, and the liberty of enjoying, free from molestation, the fortune left to me by a relation, who was well aware of the character of the man with whom I had to contend.—I appeal to the justice and humanity of the jury—a body of men, whose private judgment must be allowed to modify laws, that must be unjust, because definite rules can never apply to indefinite circumstances—and I deprecate punishment upon the man of my choice, freeing him, as I solemnly do, from the charge of seduction.]

"I did not put myself into a situation to justify a charge of adultery, till I had, from conviction, shaken off the fetters which bound me to Mr. Venables.—While I lived with him, I defy the voice of calumny to sully what is termed the fair fame of woman.—Neglected by my husband, I never encouraged a lover; and preserved with scrupulous care, what is termed my honour, at the expence of my peace, till he, who should have been its guardian, laid traps to ensnare me. From that moment I believed myself, in the sight of heaven, free—and no power on earth shall force me to renounce my resolution."

The judge, in summing up the evidence, alluded to "the fallacy of letting women plead their feelings, as an excuse for the violation of the marriage-vow. For his part, he had always determined to oppose all innovation, and the new-fangled notions which incroached on the good old rules of conduct. We did not want French principles in public or private life—and, if women were allowed to plead their feelings, as an excuse or palliation of infidelity, it was opening a flood-gate for immorality. What virtuous woman thought of her feelings?—It was her duty to love and obey the man chosen by her parents and relations, who were qualified by their experience to judge better for her, than she could for herself. As to the charges brought against the husband, they were vague, supported by no witnesses, excepting that of imprisonment in a private madhouse. The proofs of an insanity in the family, might render that however a prudent measure; and indeed the conduct of the lady did not appear that of a person of sane mind. Still such a mode of proceeding could not be justified, and might perhaps entitle the lady [in another court] to a sentence of separation from bed and board, during the joint lives of the parties; but he hoped that no Englishman would legalize adultery, by enabling the adulteress to enrich her seducer. Too many restrictions could not be thrown in the way of divorces, if we wished to maintain the sanctity of marriage; and, though they might bear a little hard on a few, very few individuals, it was evidently for the good of the whole."

CONCLUSION
BY THE EDITOR†

VERY FEW hints exist respecting the plan of the remainder of the work. I find only two detached sentences, and some scattered heads for the continuation of the story. I transcribe the whole.

I.

"Darnford's letters were affectionate; but circumstances occasioned delays, and the miscarriage of some letters rendered the reception of wished-for answers doubtful: his return was necessary to calm Maria's mind."

II.

"As Darnford had informed her that his business was settled, his delaying to return seemed extraordinary; but love to excess, excludes fear or suspicion."

The scattered heads for the continuation of the story, are as follow.*

I.

"Trial for adultery—Maria defends herself—A separation from bed and board is the consequence—Her fortune is thrown into chancery—Darnford obtains a part of his property—Maria goes into the country."

*To understand these minutes, it is necessary the reader should consider each of them as setting out from the same point in the story, *viz.* the point to which it is brought down in the preceding chapter. [Godwin's note]

†i.e., Godwin [Publisher's note].

II.

"A prosecution for adultery commenced—Trial—Darnford sets out for France—Letters—Once more pregnant—He returns—Mysterious behaviour—Visit—Expectation—Discovery—Interview—Consequence."

III.

"Sued by her husband—Damages awarded to him—Separation from bed and board—Darnford goes abroad—Maria into the country—Provides for her father—Is shunned—Returns to London—Expects to see her lover—The rack of expectation—Finds herself again with child—Delighted—A discovery—A visit—A miscarriage—Conclusion."

IV.

"Divorced by her husband—Her lover unfaithful—Pregnancy—Miscarriage—Suicide."

[The following passage appears in some respects to deviate from the preceding hints. It is superscribed]

"THE END.

"She swallowed the laudanum; her soul was calm—the tempest had subsided—and nothing remained but an eager longing to forget herself—to fly from the anguish she endured to escape from thought—from this hell of disappointment.

"Still her eyes closed not—one remembrance with frightful velocity followed another—All the incidents of her life were in arms, embodied to assail her, and prevent her sinking into the sleep of death.—Her murdered child again appeared to her, mourning for the babe of which she was the tomb.—'And could it have a nobler?—Surely it is better to die with me, than to enter on life without a mother's care!—I cannot live! —but could I have deserted my child the moment it was born? —thrown it on the troubled wave of life, without a hand to support it?'—She looked up: 'What have I not suffered!—may I find a father where I am going!'—Her head turned; a stupor

ensued; a faintness—'Have a little patience,' said Maria, hold-
ing her swimming head (she thought of her mother), 'this
cannot last long; and what is a little bodily pain to the pangs
I have endured?'

"A new vision swam before her. Jemima seemed to enter—
leading a little creature, that, with tottering footsteps, approached the bed. The voice of Jemima sounding as at a distance, called her—she tried to listen, to speak, to look!

" 'Behold your child!' exclaimed Jemima. Maria started off
the bed, and fainted.—Violent vomiting followed.

"When she was restored to life, Jemima addressed her with
great solemnity: '———— led me to suspect, that your husband and brother had deceived you, and secreted the child.
I would not torment you with doubtful hopes, and I left you
(at a fatal moment) to search for the child!—I snatched her
from misery—and (now she is alive again) would you leave her
alone in the world, to endure what I have endured?'

"Maria gazed wildly at her, her whole frame was convulsed
with emotion; when the child, whom Jemima had been tutor-
ing all the journey, uttered the word 'Mamma!' She caught
her to her bosom, and burst into a passion of tears—then,
resting the child gently on the bed, as if afraid of killing it,—
she put her hand to her eyes, to conceal as it were the agonizing struggle of her soul. She remained silent for five minutes,
crossing her arms over her bosom, and reclining her head,—
then exclaimed: 'The conflict is over!—I will live for my
child!' "

A few readers perhaps, in looking over these hints, will
wonder how it could have been practicable, without tediousness, or remitting in any degree the interest of the story, to
have filled, from these slight sketches, a number of pages,
more considerable than those which have been already presented. But, in reality, these hints, simple as they are, are
pregnant with passion and distress. It is the refuge of barren
authors only, to crowd their fictions with so great a number
of events, as to suffer no one of them to sink into the reader's

mind. It is the province of true genius to develop events, to discover their capabilities, to ascertain the different passions and sentiments with which they are fraught, and to diversify them with incidents, that give reality to the picture, and take a hold upon the mind of a reader of taste, from which they can never be loosened. It was particularly the design of the author, in the present instance, to make her story subordinate to a great moral purpose, that "of exhibiting the misery and oppression, peculiar to women, that arise out of the partial laws and customs of society.—This view restrained her fancy."* It was necessary for her, to place in a striking point of view, evils that are too frequently overlooked, and to drag into light those details of oppression, of which the grosser and more insensible part of mankind make little account.

THE END.

*See author's preface. [Godwin's note]